MW01093336

Merlin's Door

Book One of The Magic of Merlin Series

To Debbie,
Enjoy the magic!
Enjoy all the best,

Mary Troeda

Merlin's Door

Mary Triola

Quiet Storm Publishing • Martinsburg, WV

Published by Quiet Storm Publishing
PO BOX 1666
Martinsburg, WV 25402

www.quietstormpublishing.com

Cover by : Sara Lindley

ISBN: 0-9744084-3-3

Library of Congress Control Number: 2004105002

This is a work of fiction. Any resemblance to actual events or persons, living or dead, is entirely coincidental.

Printed in the United States of America

ACKNOWLEDGEMENTS

It is a true joy to work with my publisher, Clint Gaige, President of Quiet Storm Publishing. He is a man of utmost integrity and boundless energy. Clint and his faithful staff work tirelessly to produce some of the best books in the business.

Sara Lindley, a long-time friend and gifted artist, created the cover art for Merlin's Door. Her gift for expressing words in visual art shines in all her work, and particularly in her cover art for novels and other publications.

I am deeply grateful to Sean Meiers, who worked his editing magic on Merlin's Door.

I want to thank Helen Ross and Bill Reese for creating the publicity photo of me with my harp. Getting me to stand still somewhere for a photograph is a challenge in itself.

My daughter, Lauren, who is also a fantasy writer, read Merlin's Door for continuity and gave it a review of "cool," and she is a tough one to please.

My family and friends have my profoundest thanks for their unwavering support and encouragement. In particular I am indebted to Darla for her wisdom and enthusiasm.

CHAPTER ONE
The Vision

The mirror gleamed fluid silver as the girl drew closer. She picked up her brush and began to stroke it gently through the red hair that framed her strong face in flames. Three candles cast weird, wavering shadows on the walls as the flames moved with the slight breeze from the girl's movements.

A loud rap at the door roused the girl from her thoughts. "The lights are back on now," came her mother's voice from the other side. "Don't forget to blow out those candles before you go to bed."

"Okay, Mom," she answered, absently pulling the brush through her hair. She made no move to switch on the electric lights; she preferred the warm, but eerie, glow of the candles instead.

The mirror drew her gaze again. Her hands still moved, but not, it seemed, of her own volition. She began to hum to herself, a tune that she had never heard before, but now it seemed familiar as it wound its way around her thoughts and buried itself in memory. Deeper and deeper her gaze penetrated into the mirror, until she no longer saw her own reflection or was even aware of herself.

Mist trailed out of the silver surface, thickening and swirling as the girl continued to gaze, mesmerized by the sight. Then, as though a breeze had arisen, the mist parted. She could make out the figure of a woman, then two more. Their hair hung in ringlets down their backs, merging with the gossamer folds of their dresses. They peered with great interest at the blue sphere that floated between them.

"Can you see it, Amera?" one of the women asked.

The lady in the middle shook her head, her gleaming strands of silver and black hair shimmering with the movement. "No, it is not yet clear, Granuaile."

The girl felt herself drawn into the scene. Now she seemed to be standing among the three, who took no notice of her. The girl's eyes were riveted to the sphere and the scene that was unfolding there. A man lay as though asleep on a narrow bed that was draped in silver, his well-kept, long, brown locks, falling across the satin pillow on which his head rested. A sword lay lightly upon him, its jeweled hilt clasped in his hands upon his breast.

"I see him now; do you, Gran?"

"Yes. How peaceful he appears."

A shadow crept over the man's face. A slender figure in a hooded cloak stepped into the scene and stood at the man's side. For a moment it simply stood, perhaps in contemplation of the inert form.

"Who is that?" Amera whispered, a hint of fear in her soft voice.

"I do not know."

The figure raised an arm high above the sleeping man.

The young girl gasped. "It's a knife! No!" she whispered. "No! No! They have to stop it!"

The third woman spoke in raspy tones. "She who bewitched the enchanter...it is she!" The old woman passed her hand over the sphere and the scene changed. "There," she cried, "that is what she is after!"

The three women peered closely at the robed figure who now sat on a throne with her hood thrown back, revealing a beautiful and ageless face. She wore a golden circlet on her head and held a shining sword aloft while throngs of people of every nation bowed down to her. The girl noticed that many of the people trembled even as they cried out, "Long live our queen, she who has conquered the mighty!"

The woman lowered the sword and smiled upon her subjects, a terrible smile that curled with a cruelty the young girl had never before seen in her short life. "Yes," the woman murmured, "you do well to worship me in fear." Then she whispered to a huge warrior on her right and gestured toward a small group of people in the front of the crowd. The man, who wore a breastplate of leather studded with silver spikes, motioned to other guards like himself and strode toward the crowd.

Suddenly the crowd at the front dispersed, deserting the group indicated by the woman. These people wore robes and had not bowed to her. The warriors surrounded them and pushed and prodded them toward the queen.

"So," the queen began sweetly. "You do not wish to bow to me? When I have destroyed all hope?"

"There is always hope," replied a young man's voice from beneath his hooded cloak.

"But not for you," the queen retorted, the cruel smile curling her thin lips again. Turning to her warriors she commanded, "Make an example of them."

The warriors rushed into the group slashing and stabbing with their swords.

The young girl reached out toward the sphere crying, "No!" The sphere went black and dropped to the ground. The women turned to the girl. For a moment they stared at her as if trying to recognize her, then Gran smiled.

"I--I couldn't stand it!" the girl began.

"Just remember what he said: There is always hope." Then the three women vanished and the girl found herself looking at her own face in the mirror. Frightened, she ran to the light switch and turned on the overhead light. She returned to the mirror and touched it. Nothing of the vision remained. Her features relaxed.

"Just a trick of the light. Yeah, that's what it was," she whispered to herself. She picked up her brush and resumed grooming her hair. "Flickering candles can do that," she continued to reassure herself. She bent to blow them out. But she could still hear Granuaile's voice. "Remember...there is always hope." Hope? For what? Maybe she was just nervous about her math test the next day. But she shouldn't be; she had studied and, besides, math was one of her best subjects.

As she climbed into bed, she reached for the bedside lamp, and then hesitated. No, maybe it would be better to leave it on tonight. She didn't want to see that scene again. It had been horrible to watch the warriors attacking the people in robes.

It took a long time for her to finally fall asleep. The last image in her mind was of the three women looking at her from out of the mirror. How had they known she was even there?

11

CHAPTER TWO
An Odd Pair

Carter settled into the back seat of his mother's station wagon. "Don't forget your seatbelt, honey." His mom smiled sweetly at him in the rearview mirror.

"Already got it on, Mom." Sheesh! Couldn't she trust him to do anything himself?

"At least you're getting out of school," she reminded him.

Yeah, that part was nice, but he had never liked going to Great Aunt Belinda's house; it was dark and full of dusty antiques.

"I will miss her, I think," he murmured as he gazed out the window at the tree-lined hills. They were pretty, with the leaves just beginning to change colors from summer greens to fall yellows, oranges and reds.

Great Aunt B, as they used to call her, was an eccentric old lady with long, silver hair as straight and shiny as a sheet of metal. She hadn't been much of a housekeeper, but she was always particular about her antiques. "Don't touch anything you don't want to pay for," she would warn Carter. "And everything is expensive."

That kept him either sitting very still in whatever chair she approved for him or outside roaming the woods that surrounded the huge, gabled house. Carter preferred the woods. He didn't like to admit it, but he was afraid of that house. Not just because of the expensive antiques, but because there was something unsettling about the place, with its high ceilings and baffling sets of passages that sometimes seemed to go nowhere at all.

Penny was much braver than he was. He admired her for that. Nothing frightened her—and she was a girl.

Mrs. Blume looked at her son, morose in the rearview mirror. "This might be fun for you, Carter. Maybe your little friend will be around."

"Yeah, maybe so," he answered. He wished his mom wouldn't call Penny his little friend. He could hear the girl now, red curls bouncing with every word, hands on hips. "I am not little!" she would declare, but never within earshot of Mrs. Blume.

At twelve, Penny was a year older than Carter. Her mother home-schooled her and planned to do the same for her baby brother, Daryl. Penny only had to spend three or four hours a day doing schoolwork. The rest of the day was usually hers.

Carter felt vaguely jealous when he thought of that. He hated going to school. The kids bullied him because he liked science, and he knew things that even surprised his teachers.

The other boys had no appreciation for his advanced knowledge. They'd rather pound on him or throw spitballs at him. Carter put up with it, picking off the day's spitballs before going home so his mother wouldn't see. He had learned long ago that most of the teachers couldn't, or wouldn't, stop the bullies— something about not upsetting their parents.

Now, after years of uncomfortable visits with Great Aunt Belinda, she was gone. Mrs. Blume had brought her son along to help her sort through B's possessions. Carter knew he could look forward to several visits to the house over the next few months. There was a lot of stuff to go through, organize, and finally send off to whoever was named in the will. The rest would probably be sold at auction.

The best part was that he would be able to see Penny. She was one of the few people that really liked him for who he was. He tried not to think of what would happen when his mom was finished with the house. The family still had to decide whether or not to sell it. If they sold the house there would be no reason to go there and no chance of seeing his friend again. No, best not to think about that.

"Let's stop for lunch," Mrs. Blume's voice broke Carter's reverie. The car turned off the highway and onto the exit ramp. "You hungry?"

"Uh, yeah, sure," the boy answered absently. He usually spent these trips gazing out the window and wondering how people lived in the houses and farms they passed.

He didn't pay much attention to the fast food place when they pulled up, just another Burger Deluxe. But as he and his mom got out of the car, his gaze was drawn to a silver Rolls that had just turned into the parking lot after them.

"You don't see those very often," his mother commented.

"Rolls Royce Silver Shadow," Carter murmured, awestruck.

"How do you know that?"

"Oh, Uncle Mark gave me one from his model collection." Carter stared as the car was parked with care at the far end of the lot. The driver's door swung open and out stepped a gentleman wearing an impeccable, gray suit. He made his way around to the other side of the car and began to open the passenger door.

"C'mon, Carter. I'm starved." Mrs. Blume stepped into his line of sight and made for the restaurant.

"Yeah, coming," Carter replied, moving around his mom so he could see the passenger from the Rolls. He watched as the well-dressed man offered a hand to his traveling companion. Carter saw a gloved hand reach out and grasp the proffered support. A tall and elegant woman stepped out. She was completely dressed in black, from the high-heeled shoes on her feet to the black hat crowning her straight, black hair. A short veil hung in an elegant curve over her eyes. But Carter could still see the glittering light in their depths as she gazed about in an unhurried inspection of her surroundings.

When the woman looked at him the boy turned and walked quickly after his mother, who stood holding the door for him. "You shouldn't stare like that, honey. It's rude." But he noticed his mom couldn't help watching the two strangers as they headed for the restaurant either.

"C'mon, Mom." Carter tugged at her sleeve. "It's impolite to stare."

Mrs. Blume grinned sheepishly and followed him. "Guess anyone can have a hankering for fast food," she commented under her breath. She glanced back one more time before striding up to the cash register.

As they made their way to a table with their lunch, Carter and his mom witnessed the grand entrance of the peculiar couple. The man opened the door and held it for his companion, who had pulled her veil up onto her hat. Carter's eyes were irresistibly drawn to her face, ageless and smooth as fine porcelain. Her eyes were large and unusually bright. She stopped in the doorway and inspected the restaurant with an imperious gaze. In leisurely fashion the woman walked toward the cashier. Her companion followed swiftly, glancing around with an air that assured the rest of the patrons that these two were of a much higher station than the normal clientele.

"Oh, aren't we privileged," a woman muttered at a nearby table. Mrs. Blume struggled to suppress a laugh at the sarcastic remark.

"What are they doing in a place like this?" Carter asked in a whisper.

His mom shrugged. "Maybe they're from another country and they just want to see how Americans live."

The strange couple took a table in a far corner, their tray piled with food. The gentleman had to return to the front for another tray, this time loaded with drinks. The lady then proceeded to eat a prodigious amount of food. In fact, she seemed to be eating it all. Carter's jaw dropped as he watched her drink five milkshakes after downing the same number of chicken sandwiches and hamburgers.

"How can she do that?" he murmured, incredulous.

"Let's not stare, honey." But his mom didn't seem to be able to take her eyes off the unusual sight, either. Even more peculiar was the fact that the woman's partner did not consume a thing. He simply sat and watched with disinterest.

Mrs. Blume stood and picked up the tray of trash. "C'mon, Carter. We better go. I've got a lot of work ahead of me."

"Yeah," the boy replied. He followed his mother out the door, still watching the strange couple.

As they drove from the parking lot, Carter noticed the vanity plate on the Rolls. It simply read "Fate."

15

CHAPTER THREE
A Strange Request

The streets grew more familiar as they neared the house. Carter remembered playing here with Penny. There was the basketball court where she had taught him how to shoot free throws. Now they were passing her place, a comfortable two-story house with white wood siding. He liked that place a lot better than Belinda's grim mansion.

The car nosed onto the old street with a black and white sign that read "Dead End." "They were right about that," Carter muttered to himself. They passed a couple of blocks of older homes, each one bigger than the last. At the end of the street they stopped at the black iron gate.

"Would you get that for me, honey?" his mom asked.

"Sure." The boy jumped out and ran to open the gate. He waved his mom through.

"Thanks. Getting back in?"

Carter shook his head. "No, thanks. I think I'll walk up."

"Okay." The car wound up the paved driveway. Aunt Belinda had always kept the driveway free of cracks and potholes so there wouldn't be any bumps when she wanted to move her antiques or bring new ones home. Carter had often wondered if his aunt would ever stop buying antiques. It seemed that she always had a new one to show off every time they had come for a visit.

Mrs. Blume parked the car and got out. She waved at him before opening her purse to look for the house keys. Carter made his way up the drive. Suddenly a huge raven called from the tree next to him. Startled, the boy broke into a run. The bird flung itself into the air and flapped alongside him. Carter ran faster. The raven

16

made a sound that seemed almost a laugh before it turned and flew off into the distance.

"Did you see that?" Carter called to his mom as he slowed to a walk in front of the steps.

"See what?" Mrs. Blume pulled a set of keys out of her purse. "Aha! There they are!"

"Uh, just a big bird. Nothing important."

"Now to see if these work," his mom said as she slid a key into the deadbolt lock above the door handle. She turned it and heard the bolt slide back. "Well, that one worked. Let's see about this one." She put another key into the polished lock of the handle. With one, smooth movement she turned it and pushed the door open.

"Our lock doesn't do that," Carter observed.

"Well, Aunt B had to have good locks to protect all of her things." She stepped into the house. "Stuffy in here."

The boy hung back as the powerful scent of antique woods and upholstery rushed out the door to meet him like so many ghosts. He wrinkled his nose and hunched his shoulders.

"C'mon in, honey." Mrs. Blume flipped a switch and looked around the foyer. White plaster walls glowed pale yellow in the light from the chandelier. The dark wood floor shone with a recent polish.

Carter walked into the house. At any moment he expected his great aunt to come down the huge staircase before him and warn him not to touch anything. Mrs. Blume hung her jacket on the iron coat rack by the door, turned to the right and walked into the large parlor, the boy still at her side. Kicking off her shoes she sank her toes into the thick, red Persian rug. "Ooh," she sighed. "I've always wanted to do that!"

She sat down on a velvet-covered divan and pulled some papers out of her tote bag. "I guess I'll start with this room." Glancing up, she noticed her son standing uncomfortably at the edge of the rug. "Do you want to watch T.V.?"

"Uh, sure. I can do that." T.V. sounded safe. He turned and walked back across the foyer to the den where he had often taken refuge so he wouldn't disturb Aunt Belinda's antiques.

17

Carter settled into an overstuffed chair and flipped through the channels. Nothing looked very interesting. Just as he was about to turn the T.V. off he heard a loud rapping at the front door.

"Would you get that, Carter?" his mom called. "It's probably your little friend."

Little friend—hope Penny didn't hear that, he thought as he got up and hurried to the door. He smiled, glad his friend had come over so quickly. But the smile froze on his face when he opened the door and saw the strange couple from the Burger Deluxe.

A vague look of half-surprise crossed the gentleman's features for a moment, before it cleared and was replaced by stiff formality. "Good day, young sir. Are you a relative of Miss Feltree's?"

"Who? Oh, Aunt B. Uh, yeah, I mean, yes. She's my great aunt."

Mrs. Blume hurried to Carter's side and peered out over her son's shoulder. "May I help you?" her polite tone barely hiding her annoyance at this intrusion. She tried not to stare when she recognized them.

"Good day, Madam. I wish to extend our condolences to your family."

"Thank you." Carter's mom nudged him aside and stepped forward into a protective stance. Her voice had taken on a wary tone. "Is there a problem?"

"No, no problem, Madam. We are antique dealers of Miss Feltree's acquaintance."

Oh, boy, the vultures had descended. Mrs. Blume wondered what could be so important that these two would come so quickly after her aunt's death. She had just been buried last week. Now this strange duo stood at the door wanting something that Aunt Belinda had. Maybe she should turn them away before they said another word.

"I will be brief. Miss Feltree had an antique door in her possession. It is a cumbersome thing. We thought that we could relieve you of the burden of having to move it from the house and finding a buyer." He leaned forward, the white tips of his teeth glinting in the sunlight. "We will pay very handsomely for it."

18

"You will, huh?" Mrs. Blume shook her head. "Look, I haven't even started going through her things yet. I don't even know if she has the door, much less what she wanted us to do with it."

She placed a hand on Carter's shoulder and pushed him behind her, out of the doorway. "You'll just have to come back another time and ask, maybe in another month or two." She put both hands on the door, intending to shut it.

The gentleman stepped forward and gave her a little bow. "I'm so sorry to have disturbed you. We are only in the country for a fortnight." He reached into the inside pocket of his jacket and brought out a business card. Handing it to Mrs. Blume with another bow, he added, "Our hotel number is on this. Would you be so kind as to call us as soon as possible about the piece?"

She took the card and glanced at it. "Okay, if I find this door and figure out what I'm supposed to do with it, I'll give you a call."

"Thank you, Madam." He stepped back as Carter's mom closed the door. The boy hurried to the window in time to see the woman hit her partner with her purse. As they walked toward the car, she looked as though she were scolding the gentleman, who seemed to take it very meekly.

Mrs. Blume watched the odd conflict at the other window. "What is that all about?" she muttered. "He should drive off and leave the old bat on the side of the road."

Unperturbed, the gentleman opened the door for his partner, who continued her scolding even after he had closed her door and walked around to the driver's side. He got in the car and drove off.

Mrs. Blume shook her head. "Weird!"

"What's on the card?" Carter asked, coming up beside her.

She handed it to him. It read: "Nimway and Stonehurst, Dealers in Fine Antiques, in the U.S. and the U.K." The name and number of a local bed and breakfast was handwritten in careful script at the bottom.

Carter didn't have long to ponder over the card. A couple of quick rings of the doorbell told him that Penny had arrived. She always rang like that. He flashed a smile at his mom. "There she is!" he exclaimed as he stepped to the door and pulled it open.

CHAPTER FOUR
An Ancient Door

"Hi, Penny." Carter tried to hide his excitement at seeing his friend.

Penny's red curls bounced with enthusiasm. Carter liked how they glowed in the sunlight like strands of jewels hung about the girl's round face. "Hi! Who were those weird people in the limo?"

"It wasn't a limo it was a Rolls Royce. I dunno. They want some door my great aunt had." Remembering his manners he opened the door wide and gestured for Penny to come in the house.

"Hello, Penny," Mrs. Blume called from the parlor, where she had resumed her seat on the divan. "How is your family doing?"

"Just fine, Mrs. Blume." The girl walked across the foyer and sat down on the Persian rug as comfortable as if she were in her own home. Carter envied that about her.

"Do you like having a baby brother?" his mom asked.

"Yeah, it's okay. I take care of him sometimes. I think he'll be more fun when he can walk."

"Then you can take him on some of your adventures."

Penny grinned. "Only if he can keep up!"

Mrs. Blume laughed. "He'll have to!" Her face became serious as another thought crossed her mind. She looked at her son. "Carter, maybe you and Penny could look around for that door."

The boy shrugged. "I guess we could. What's it look like?"

"I don't know...old. I haven't found it mentioned in the will and I read it over a few times before we left."

"Door?" Penny looked questioningly from one to the other. "We can look," she assured Mrs. Blume.

20

"Thanks. Oh, and Carter, would you bring in the stuff we brought? Those drinks need to go in the 'fridge. You and Penny can help yourselves, too."

"Okay." He turned to Penny, who jumped up off the floor, ready for action. "Mind helping me?"

"Nope," she answered and followed him out the door.

The two carried the cooler into the kitchen and returned to the car for a large box of packing materials. "How long you going to stay?" Penny asked.

"Over the weekend. Mom took me out of school for the day. I think we'll go back Sunday afternoon."

"Oh, cool! That gives us a couple of days to hang out."

"Want a soda?"

Penny nodded. "Sure, thanks."

Carter handed her a can and took one for him. "So, think we should start looking in the attic?"

His friend opened her can and took a sip. "We've been up there hundreds of times. We've never seen a door."

"Uh, are you sure it couldn't be up there? I mean, it's a huge attic. Maybe we should check again."

Penny shot him an impatient glance. "No. I think we should look in the basement."

The boy's face paled. He swallowed hard. "The...the basement?"

"Y...yeah," she teased. "What's wrong with the basement?" A mischievous light glinted in her eyes. "You don't believe those stories, do you?"

"Stories? What stories?" Carter looked down nervously, as though something terrible might come up right through the floor.

"You do believe them!"

"I do not! There's no such thing as ghosts or haunted antiques..." but he trailed off, unconvinced.

Penny smiled, trying to reassure him. "I don't believe in them either. Besides, I've been dying to explore your aunt's basement. They say there's a lot of weird stuff down there."

Mrs. Blume walked into the kitchen just then. "I'm going out to pick up a few things at the store." She opened the freezer to assess its contents. "Want to come?"

Carter shook his head. "No thanks."

21

"Okay." Mrs. Blume checked the refrigerator. "Want anything besides those frozen dinners you like?"

"Double chocolate fudge ice cream," he answered.

His mother smiled. "If they have it." She rummaged in her purse. "Have either of you seen my keys?"

Without looking up Carter pointed to the refrigerator. "Up there."

Mrs. Blume reached up and grabbed them with a laugh. "Good thing you know where I put things, honey, or I'd never get anywhere." She bent down and kissed him on the top of the head. Penny giggled when he blushed in embarrassment. "Now you kids be careful while I'm gone."

"Sure, Mom. Don't worry."

"Yeah, I'll protect him from all the scary ghosts around here," Penny added with a smirk.

"There aren't any ghosts," the boy protested.

"Right. Have fun." Mrs. Blume turned and left the room. They could hear her close the front door and pull on it to make sure it locked.

"Of course there aren't any ghosts. They're all too scared of your Great Aunt Belinda and what she kept down in the basement."

Carter set his can on the table. He glanced at his friend. "Well," he began, gathering his courage. "Let's go find that door."

The pair headed toward the basement. Carter opened the door, and then hesitated at the top of the steps. "What's up?" Penny asked with a quizzical look.

"Uh, nothing," the boy stammered, blushing.

She tossed her head. "Don't worry. I'll go first."

"I wasn't worried about that," he muttered to himself, unconvinced of any truth in those words.

Penny tripped down the stairs in the light of the bare bulb overhead. Carter followed slowly behind her, glancing fearfully around him as he reached the bottom of the steps.

His companion had already managed to find the various switches that turned on the rest of the lights in the huge basement. She began to methodically look around the antiques that were stacked from floor to ceiling. Carter tried to relax and focus on the task at hand.

22

Penny pointed off to her right. "Why don't you check over there?" He nodded and peered around the piles that included tables, chairs—with and without legs—trunks, and odd statuary. He was glad that his aunt had installed several lights. There were very few deep shadows from which some terrible, ghostly creature could spring at him. He smiled at the cuckoo clock with a bird in a clown suit. Maybe his aunt had possessed a sense of humor after all.

Still grinning he turned to see a frightening creature glaring down at him from the top of a tall set of shelves. He caught his breath and clapped his hand over his mouth to stifle a scream. The creature fixed him in its frightening gaze, green scales shimmering in the shadowy light, red eyes gleaming like coals.

Carter turned and ran back to where he had left Penny. He didn't see her. "Penny!" he whispered urgently. "Penny!"

His friend stepped out from behind a wardrobe of dark cherry wood. "What's the matter?" He pointed back the way he had come. For a moment he could not speak.

"Did you see a ghost or something?" Penny looked amused.

"Some…some horrible thing over there…with red eyes, and it looked at me!"

"So your aunt is hiding monsters down here?" She walked boldly in the direction Carter had indicated. "I can't wait to see it! I've never seen a monster before."

Carter followed, hanging back at a safe distance. He wanted to be able to run away if he had to. Looking up he glimpsed the creature again. "There it is," he whispered, stepping back. Afraid to even see it, he backed away, glancing around him to be sure there were no other strange beings ready to pounce on him.

Penny stood, hands on hips, staring at the gargoyle. "It's kind of cute, you know."

"Cute?"

"Yeah, but it's just one of those garden statues. No eyes glaring at me or anything like that."

Carter stayed back, just in case the thing wanted to come to life again. "Hey! What are you doing?"

Penny had stepped up to the shelf and begun to climb. "I want a closer look."

"Closer look? You're crazy! That thing—it was really alive..." He trailed off, knowing that nothing he said could stop her. He felt afraid for her but he noticed that part of him felt proud of her boldness, proud that she was his friend.

Penny gazed, perplexed, straight into the gargoyle's eyes. "I don't see why your aunt would want this. It really is just a cheap garden statue. Nothing special at all about it." Holding tightly onto the wood support with one hand, she reached out with the other to touch it. "It feels like plaster or something." The girl picked it up by an outstretched wing.

"This is really light. Maybe it went in her garden. Do you remember seeing it there?"

Carter stepped gingerly out of hiding to stand by the shelves under Penny. "I don't know. She had lots of weird statues in the garden. It could be one of them. She did bring them in the house for the winter."

Penny began to set it down when, suddenly, she lost her grip on the wood support. She let go of the statue and grabbed for the shelf with her other hand. The gargoyle bounced on the edge of the shelf and plummeted to the floor, shattering into pieces. "Oh, no! I'm so sorry!" Penny exclaimed in dismay.

Carter yelled in fright as he watched a small, gray shadow emerge from the head of the broken gargoyle and scurry away. "There...there was something inside it!"

"What?" Penny jumped down from the shelf. "Something's inside it?"

He nodded, eyes wide. "A shadowy, gray thing."

"Where?" Penny bent to examine the pieces.

"It's gone now. It ran away."

"Maybe a ghost lived inside it!" She grinned and patted him on the head. "It's okay, Carter. It was probably just a mouse. The fall must have scared it out of its hole."

"Yeah, you're probably right," he agreed, but he sounded doubtful.

Penny brushed her hands on her jeans and looked around the basement room. "Which way did it go, anyway?"

Carter pointed off into the shadows. "That way, toward the door."

Penny nodded. "We'll explore there next. But I want to check out those costumes your aunt has over here."

She turned and walked back to the piles of boxes and trunks she had been investigating before Carter called her to see the gargoyle. "Wow! These are great costumes!" she exclaimed, digging once more into a large trunk. She pulled out a black robe. "This is cool! Want to try it on?"

Carter shook his head. He was more intrigued by the glimpses of weapons and armor he had noticed in another section. The light from the bare bulb reflected off the metal with an eerie glow. Though fearful, the boy drew nearer to the wall where he saw a large display of swords, spears, maces and halberds. "Did you see these?" he called to Penny. He reached out and touched the blade on a halberd. "This looks like an axe or something." He ran his finger along the edge. "Ow!" he exclaimed, pulling his finger back and popping it in his mouth. The blood had a metallic taste. "That's really sharp!" He glanced toward the area where he had left Penny. She wasn't there. "Penny?" he called, fear rising in prickles up his spine. His voice dropped to a whisper. "Penny?"

Carter stepped cautiously toward the trunk of costumes. It lay open but his friend was nowhere in sight. "Hey, this isn't funny. Where are you?" He swallowed hard. First the strange gargoyle and now Penny had disappeared. Was he next? Now he began to worry more about his friend than his own safety as he moved slowly back to the shelves Penny had climbed. Maybe she had gone back there to check out that stuff. He had noticed a lot of other statues on the shelves.

"Penny?" He glanced around, checking over his shoulder every once in a while. Ahead of him stood a door. He wondered if she had gone through it into another room. He took a deep breath and moved toward it. The door was very old, probably another of his aunt's antiques. The wood looked shiny with wear around the wooden handle. Around the edges bits of wood had come off as the door had deteriorated over the years. As Carter reached for the handle he heard a step behind him.

He turned and saw a tall figure in a black, hooded cloak. He gasped as fear gripped him. Without another thought he grabbed the door handle and pulled it with all his might. Suddenly Carter realized the door was not attached to the wall. There was no room

25

behind it. He jumped out of the way as it fell toward him. He heard the crash and splinter of wood as he ran into a darker section of basement. He stumbled over chairs and ran into boxes, knocked over at least one lamp and a hat stand before he finally stopped at the cinderblock wall. There was nowhere else to run. He was trapped. He turned to face the dark figure but lost his balance and fell sideways into a pile of boxes and plastic bags full of who-knows-what.

Carter pulled the bags over him in an attempt to hide. He panted with fear and the exertion. Had the figure followed him? He peered out from his hiding place. There it was, standing there. It looked like it was shaking. Suddenly a hand reached up and threw back the hood. Red hair and Penny's laughing face appeared. The girl shook with the loud laughter that she had tried to suppress.

"You should have seen your face!" Penny exclaimed, giggling and putting a hand over her mouth. "Boy! Were you scared!"

Carter could feel his cheeks grow hot with embarrassment. He glared at his friend. She knew how scared he was to be down here. She didn't have to do that, he thought. Suddenly he remembered the door that had crashed to the floor when he pulled on it. He stood up, the bags tumbling around him. "That door...do you think..." He hurried back the way he had come.

Penny followed. "You pulled it away from the wall so hard. I guess you're stronger than I thought. It broke, right down the middle."

Carter ran over to what was left of the door. It had fallen onto a large, stone statue of a satyr and broken length-wise down the middle. Now, the halves lay against either side of the sculpture. One of the satyr's horns lay on the floor at its feet. The boy gasped.

"Now you're in for it," Penny murmured behind him.

"Maybe it's not the one they were looking for. It doesn't look very special..." But inside he knew he was wrong.

Penny shook her head. "Knowing your luck... This is the only old door we've found so far."

A faint tremor shook the basement. Carter stiffened. "Did you feel that?"

"Probably just that construction going on behind the houses."

"What are they building?" The tremors grew stronger.

"Uh, another shopping center." Penny glanced around. Carter backed away from the broken door. The basement shook so hard that a lamp fell off the shelf behind him. He jumped. "That's no construction I've ever heard." Penny nodded. "Maybe it's an earthquake. Let's get out of here."

Carter knew there weren't any earthquakes around there but he didn't care about the explanation as he turned to run out of the basement. Penny, about to follow him, gasped suddenly. The boy looked back at Penny, who stood frozen in fear, gazing at the splintered door. He followed her gaze.

Streams of multicolored light shot from the broken edges while the floor and walls trembled all around them. Their ears were filled with a rumble like thunder rolling back and forth throughout the room. The light gathered into a cloud that filled the basement. It turned from red to orange to yellow, then green, blue and finally violet.

The children stood still, staring with mouths open in wonder as well as terror. The light began to take human shape. Eyes began to emerge in a sparkling blue from beneath a cloud of white eyebrows. The beard flowed like a drift of snow down the deep purple robe of embroidered velvet.

The figure raised his arms and spoke in a language that Carter did not recognize. He glanced at Penny. "Latin," she whispered.

"Can he see us?" Carter whispered back.

"Of course." The voice rumbled slowly in the old man's chest. "I am not blind. I have just been asleep."

Penny, now fully recovered from the shock, took a step forward. "Who are you?"

The eyes peered at her for a moment, then moved to inspect her companion. "It has been a very long time, then, if you do not know me." He stroked his soft beard. "My name is Merlin."

CHAPTER FIVE
Merlin

"Merlin?" Penny sounded skeptical. "I thought he was under some sort of spell in England."

"Maybe you shouldn't say that to a wizard," Carter cautioned.

"I prefer enchanter or magician," the old man commented, "or perhaps even mage. Yes, I like the sound of that, too." He bent his head in what appeared to be deep thought.

Seeing the enchanter was no longer speaking to them, Carter edged back another step. "Well, it was nice to meet you but we really better be going."

Penny grabbed him by the shoulder. "What are you talking about? We just see the most amazing thing and you want to leave?"

Merlin raised his head. "Conversation, ah, yes. I was talking to you. People expect one to keep the conversation flowing in a continuous fashion. My deepest apologies."

"It's okay." Penny cocked her head and studied the figure. "Aren't you supposed to be in a forest in England?"

"England? Oh, Britain. I was. But now...I am here." He turned and looked at the broken door. "Given that this door is broken, my tree must have been cut down and made into a useful article and brought...here...wherever here is."

"America," Carter offered in a helpful voice. "What do you mean by your tree?"

The old man smiled. "You are not familiar with my story, then."

"I remember something about a spell...and Arthur sleeping until England needs him again." The boy gave him a sheepish look, shrugging his shoulders. "There are so many different versions of the legends that it's hard to keep track of them all."

"No matter," the enchanter said. "A jealous tree spirit lured me into a tree and trapped me there." He shook his head. "I was a little, shall we say, careless that day."

"Did you know you were there?" Penny asked.

"Yes and no. I experienced an awareness of the tree, the wood surrounding me, and at the same time, a sort of deep sleep."

"Almost like one of those dreams you can't wake up from," the girl added.

"Yes, very much like that, child."

Penny, who would usually object strenuously to anyone who called her a child, did not seem to mind it when Merlin called her that.

Merlin fixed Carter with a penetrating gaze. The boy felt almost as though the magician could see through him. He looked down at the floor.

"You were going to tell me about this 'America'", Merlin reminded him.

Carter raised his head. "Oh, yeah. We're in the United States of America."

"He doesn't know what that means," Penny interjected. If he couldn't explain she could. "Well, a bunch of English people came across the Atlantic Ocean and found this continent. They settled, even though there were some native peoples already here. More and more people came from Europe and then some of them brought slaves from Africa and before you knew it the whole country was full of—"

Merlin held up a hand. "Pardon me, but you said they came across the Atlantic Ocean and found a new continent? This is news indeed!" He stroked his beard. "So, what people are in power here?"

"Why, everyone. We have a democracy. That's when—"

"Yes, yes, I know what a democracy is. I have studied my Plato and Aristotle." He gazed absently up at the ceiling. "Oh! That is not torchlight or candlelight!" The old man stared in wonder at the bare light bulb.

29

"No, it's electricity." Penny walked over to the switch. She turned the light in that part of the basement off, then on. Merlin gasped.

"By what magic is that done?"

"No magic," the girl answered. "Just electrons moving through a copper wire."

"I remember reading of such things, but that was a very primitive technology."

"Talk of...electricity?" Carter stammered.

The old man nodded, still a little awed by the light. "Yes, talk of strange vases that held power to create light. But this light could not be produced by such a weak power source."

Penny smiled. "You mean those ancient batteries that archaeologists have found in Egypt and Greece and other places. They put grape juice and copper into a vase and could use the energy, the electricity. I wrote a term paper about it last year." The girl looked very pleased with herself.

Merlin stepped forward and put his hand on the switch. He glanced at Penny. "May I?"

"Sure. Give it a try." She stepped back to take in the complete picture of the ancient man turning the light on and off, over and over again. Carter moved closer to them, no longer afraid. Now he was just curious.

"I knew such devices would eventually be made by humans. They are clever beings, indeed." Merlin turned to Penny. "How many years have passed?"

"Well, since you are just supposed to be a legend," Penny shrugged, "we don't know."

"Legend..." the old man mused, alternately stroking his beard and switching the light on and off. "It must be a very long time. How do you count your years these days?"

"'S'cuse me?" the girl asked.

"From what point in time do you determine the passage of the years, centuries and so on?"

Carter peered quizzically into Merlin's face. "Do you mean like B.C. and A.D.?"

"What are those?"

Now the boy looked confused. Penny piped up. "B.C. stands for 'before Christ'. A.D. means Anno Domini."

Carter glanced with admiration at his friend. "I forgot you were studying Latin with your mom this year."

Merlin fixed him with an astonished stare. "You mean you have not begun your Latin, boy?"

"Uh, well...no." Carter's face reddened as though he had just gotten an answer wrong in school.

"They don't usually study Latin in school anymore. All our books are in modern English now." Penny could feel the boy's discomfort. She put a hand on his shoulder.

The enchanter nodded slowly. "Of course. How clever. I must see this new world. Which way?" Penny pointed at the stairs. He turned and began walking, with Carter and the girl behind him.

"Uh, Merlin." Penny hurried to catch up to him. She pulled on a long, purple sleeve. The enchanter stopped and looked down at her.

"Yes?"

"You can't very well go out like that. I mean, no one dresses like that anymore." Penny rubbed the material between her fingers. It felt thick and soft. Violet-colored ivy had been embroidered up and down the robe and along the edges of the sleeves.

Carter pointed to Merlin's beard. "And no one wears a beard like that, either."

"Hmm..." the old eyes twinkled with a mischievous light. "Then, do they dress like this?" Suddenly he disappeared. The voice continued to roll out of thin air. "Or does no one practice the ancient art of invisibility anymore?"

"H...how did you do that?" Carter gasped.

Merlin appeared again before them. "Why, I wouldn't be worth my salt as a magician if I couldn't become invisible. It's a basic skill." He chuckled at the children's astonishment. "Now, will you show me this world?"

Penny grinned. "With pleasure."

Carter, who had hurried up the stairs first to see if his mom had returned, stepped cautiously into the kitchen. He looked around, and then moved to the window. His mother's car was still gone. Good. She wasn't home yet. Maybe they would have time to figure out what to do with their strange guest. He turned back to the basement door.

"All clear. You can come out now. She's not back yet."

Penny gestured for Merlin to go first. "This is the kitchen," she informed him.

The old man entered the room, gazing about with interest. He nodded. "Yes, I thought as much. Ingenious, really." He moved to the sink. Penny turned the water on and off.

"Hot is on the left, cold on the right." She stood aside so he could try.

Merlin tried each faucet, holding his hand under the streams of water. He pulled it away quickly when the water became hot. A bemused smile spread over his features. He turned to the range. "Does this produce heat for cooking?"

Penny nodded. "That's a stove and this is the oven," she added, opening the oven door for him to see inside. "You turn it on with these dials here."

"Ah, very good. And you are well versed in the culinary arts?"

"Uh, well, not really." The girl's face reddened. "I don't like to cook."

"One day you will have to, unless you have servants," Merlin commented dryly.

"You're saying that because I'm a girl. But men can cook, too."

The enchanter nodded. "Of course. But I did not say it because you are a girl. I am saying it because you will need to eat."

"Oh." Penny tossed her head and walked to the refrigerator. Opening the door she gestured to the bottles of milk on the top shelf. "This keeps food cold."

Merlin moved to the appliance. He put his hand inside and held it there a moment. "Yes, very good. Nice and cold." He bent and examined the contents of the refrigerator, which included several cans of soda, a bottle of orange juice, and a block of Monterey jack cheese.

"And we keep stuff frozen up here." Penny pointed to the freezer door over his head.

Merlin straightened and reached for the handle. "May I?"

The girl nodded. Opening the freezer compartment, the old man stared at the trays of ice and the few packages of frozen food. "You hungry?" Penny asked.

"Hmm, good question. Actually, I think I would like something to eat."

Penny grabbed the only frozen dinner and opened the package. Carter watched the enchanter's reaction as she popped it in the microwave and set the timer. Merlin peered in the glass door, watching the plate of food turn on the carousel inside the oven.

"It is cooking like this? What causes the heat?"

"Microwaves," the boy answered.

"Microwaves?"

Just then the oven beeped. "That's what cooks the food so fast." Penny opened the door and placed the plastic dish on the table. She peeled back the cover. "Hey, Carter, why don't you get a fork for him?"

The boy reached into a drawer, pulled out a fork and handed it to the astounded magician. Carter gestured for him to sit at the table.

"What kind of food is this?" Merlin asked as he seated himself and rolled his capacious sleeves out of the way.

"Uh, chicken a la king." Carter sniffed the meal hungrily, realizing he wouldn't mind having one himself.

"Then you still have kings in your democratic society?"

"No. It's just what we call that particular dish." Penny answered, placing a glass of juice in front of him. She sat down next to the ancient man.

Merlin scooped up a bite of food with his fork. He eyed it curiously for a moment, and then brought it to his lips. "Hmm." He chewed thoughtfully. "This is strange food, but it does taste good."

"Glad you like it." Carter felt happy to have pleased the old enchanter.

All of a sudden Penny stood up, her eyes glued to the window. "Your mom's home!"

"Uh oh!" Carter glanced out to see his mother just opening the car door. He looked back at Merlin but the enchanter was gone. "Where...?" But then he knew what had happened. He felt a large hand on his shoulder. It propelled him into the chair where Merlin had been sitting just a moment before.

"Sit," the old man commanded quietly.

The boy nodded and sat, awed by the powers of this magician. "Right."

"Now, eat."

Carter nodded again and picked up the fork. Penny glanced around the kitchen to make sure the magician could not be seen. Then she crossed to the door and opened it for Mrs. Blume with a smile that belied all that had occurred during the shopping trip.

"Thank you, Penny." Carter's mother stepped into the house with two bags of groceries. She stopped when she saw her son. "So, you found that last dinner."

"Yup. Guess I was hungrier than I thought." The boy took another bite and chewed noisily.

"That's my growing boy," Mrs. Blume commented as she set the groceries on the shelf. Carter blushed but continued eating with what he hoped looked like good appetite.

"I had to get a different brand of ice cream," Mrs. Blume said as she carried it and four dinners to the freezer.

"Uh, great," Carter answered absently. His gaze was drawn to the second bag of groceries. It had opened by itself and a package of gum had floated out of it. Penny noticed, too. She hurried to the bag and grabbed the gum from the invisible hand.

Mrs. Blume smiled at Penny. "You can have a pack, if you like."

"Uh, thanks." Penny opened the package and pulled out one of the individual packs. She slipped it into her pocket and looked back just in time to see a box of cookies rise out of the bag. She grabbed that, too, hoping that Merlin caught the quick glare she had directed into the air in front of her.

"No, that's for later, dear." Mrs. Blume looked at Penny, surprised at her unusual behavior.

"Uh, sure. Just want to help out." The girl's face turned bright red, clashing with her copper hair.

"Well, Carter should be helping instead of sitting there eating while we do all the work."

The boy immediately jumped to his feet. "Right. Sorry, Mom." He hurried to Penny's side and reached for the other bag. His fist rammed right into something soft that grunted when he hit it.

"What was that?" his mother asked.

Carter tried to grunt just like Merlin. "Oh, nothing, Mom."

Mrs. Blume fixed him with a questioning gaze. An almost wistful expression replaced it. "I guess your voice is starting to change."

The boy wished it were true. The kids at school made fun of his high-pitched tones. One more reason for them to tease him. A lot of the other boys had lower voices already. His dad kept telling him it was a Blume trait. "Squeaky when we're young, basses when we're older. My dad had a low voice just like mine. But we both sang soprano in the boys' choir."

Soprano! Yeah, he'd sung soprano, but not in church choir. Just when the bullies cornered him and held him over the toilet, threatening to dunk him in it. Yeah, he'd sung then, hoping someone would come to his rescue. Usually they did...

Merlin must have moved off to a spot where he wouldn't get in the way because Penny and Carter didn't run into him while they finished putting the groceries away. Mrs. Blume didn't notice anything strange as she stood at the sink washing apples.

"Penny, how would you like to spend the night here? You can have the room next to Carter's. I'm sure he'd appreciate the company, if it's alright with your mom."

The girl grinned. "Thanks! I'm sure it is but I'll go home and ask. And I can pick up my things." She turned toward the kitchen door, then stopped and stared out the window. "It looks like you have another visitor."

CHAPTER SIX
Uncle Mortimer

"It can't be," Carter heard his mom mutter under her breath, "not after all these years." She hurried out of the kitchen. Carter leaned over the sink to get a better look out the window. A pale, skinny man with long dark hair made his way along the stone walk and up to the door.

"Do you know who that is?" Penny asked.

The boy shook his head. "Guess I'll go find out." He started out of the kitchen.

"Well, let me know later. I've got to go. Mom wanted me home fifteen minutes ago. Uh...Carter."

The boy turned on his heel. "What?"

Penny pointed at the open refrigerator door. "And keep an eye on him, too."

"Hey! Close that, please!" Carter whispered to his invisible guest. The door swung closed.

Penny giggled. "See ya'" she said as she shut the kitchen door behind her.

"Yeah," Carter murmured to himself. With a last glance at Penny, who was halfway down the driveway, he hurried toward the front door.

"Come in," his mother was saying to the visitor, a mixture of wonder and caution in her tones.

"Thank you," the man answered in a deep voice that sounded like it came straight out of a horror movie, one of those old movies Carter had watched late at night with his dad.

The boy hung back behind his mother, staring at the stranger. He had skin so pale it had a bluish cast to it. His hair looked scraggly and as black as shiny coal. Carter wondered if he ever ate, he seemed so thin.

Mrs. Blume turned to her son. "This is my Uncle Mortimer. He's Aunt B's brother."

The gaunt man extended a hand toward Carter. Hesitatingly, the boy took it. It was cold and clammy. Mortimer's handshake reminded him of a dead fish. "So nice to meet you. You must be Carter."

"I...I didn't know Aunt Belinda had a brother." The boy pulled his hand back and edged away. He didn't think he could like his great uncle, especially since he'd never known about him. Why hadn't his great aunt mentioned him before? Something just didn't seem right about this strange, new relative.

"Well, come into the parlor and make yourself at home." Mrs. Blume gestured toward a red, satin-covered chair. She took a seat opposite him on the divan. "I'm so sorry I couldn't reach you after Aunt B died, but there was no address for you, not even in her address book."

Mortimer smiled thinly. "It's not your fault. I've been...away."

Yeah, for at least eleven years, Carter thought. He had no recollection of this man. He wasn't even in any of his baby pictures. And everyone had come to see him when he was born. He was his mother's first child, after all. He remembered with a certain satisfaction that hardly any relatives had come to see his little sister after her birth. There was something special about being the first-born. Of course, Peggy was spoiled because she was the youngest, "the baby". He sighed. Maybe being first-born wasn't so special after all.

Carter sat on the rug, gazing around the room with its dark wood furniture. He tuned out his mother's conversation about the funeral. His eyes fell on the marble mantel over the fireplace. A goblet, one of his aunt's silver ones, began to float in the air. It turned upside down then twirled slowly around. Merlin! Carter glanced at his mother. She was facing away from the fireplace. Mortimer seemed to be looking only at her. Or could he see this phenomenon out of the corner of his eye?

Suddenly the boy coughed violently. "Are you okay?" his mother asked.

"Uh, yeah." He coughed again, hoping Merlin had gotten the signal. He tried to glimpse the goblet at the edge of his peripheral vision. It hung motionless, but still in the air. Carter got up. "I think I better go to the kitchen and get a drink." He pretended to choke on some dust. When he glanced back again he saw that the goblet once again sat on the mantel.

"Yes, that's a good idea," Mrs. Blume agreed.

The boy felt Uncle Mortimer's eyes almost boring into him as he started from the room. The long face remained expressionless except for a strange glint in his eyes. Had he seen the floating cup? Carter hurried to the kitchen, hoping that Merlin would follow him.

He breathed a sigh of relief when he heard the magician's whisper behind him. "So sorry. But I thought I recognized that goblet."

Carter turned toward the sound in the relative safety of the kitchen. "It's a replica of a medieval goblet, not a real one," he whispered back. "You can't let them see anything weird. Besides, my uncle gives me the creeps. Who knows what would happen if he found out that something strange was going on."

Merlin appeared briefly. Carter could only see his head and part of his shoulders hovering in the air in front of him. "Of course, you are correct. I shall be more careful." He flickered out of sight at the sound of Mrs. Blume's voice.

"Carter? Are you all right in there?" His mother walked into the kitchen, concern on her face. "Did you get a drink?"

Carter grabbed a cup from the cupboard overhead. "I'm getting one, Mom. Don't worry about me. I'll be just fine."

"Good." Mrs. Blume turned and started back down the hall.

"Your uncle is rather odd to me, too," Merlin whispered, nudging the boy with what must have been his invisible elbow. "Something...but it has been so long. I may not remember properly."

"Remember what?" Carter asked.

"Nothing, really. Just that there are certain energies that surround those of strong faerie blood..." He trailed off.

"Faerie blood?" The boy felt prickles on the back of his neck. "What are you talking about?" But Merlin had no time to answer. Mrs. Blume was calling to her son.

"Carter? Can you come back in here please?"

"Coming!" The boy glanced around the kitchen. "Please," he whispered urgently. "Please don't let them know you're here."

"I won't," came the answer as Carter turned and made his way back to the parlor.

Uncle Mortimer smiled, maybe as warmly as he could, Carter thought. If he had seen the floating goblet he certainly gave no indication. "Then you have recovered, nephew?"

The boy started at the term as though it couldn't possibly be true. "Uh, yeah. I'm fine—just needed a drink..." he mumbled.

"Uncle Mortimer is asking about a door, probably the same one those antique dealers were looking for." Mrs. Blume shook her head. "I don't remember any mention of it in the will. Of course, I'm sure your sister would have wanted you to have it." Mortimer nodded. "The thing may not even be here, but the kids were looking around for it today." She turned to Carter. "Did you happen to see it when you and Penny were exploring?"

Carter froze. He hoped his great uncle couldn't see the truth in the expression on his face. How could he explain what had happened? At the very least his mother would want to kill him for breaking the thing. And then there was Merlin. He shrugged and tried to look casual. "There are lots of doors in this house. It could be any one of them, I suppose."

"Well, you're right about that," his mother agreed.

Whew! He'd gotten off the hook so far, but sooner or later his mother would find out about the broken door, unless... His mind whirled as a sudden plan struck him. Of course! Penny could help him, too. She was good at getting out of scrapes.

He felt relieved when he heard the doorbell. He figured it would be Penny before he opened it. "Boy, am I glad you're here!" he muttered half to himself.

Penny grinned. "Having too much fun without me, huh?"

The two hurried up the stairs to the guest rooms. Carter held the door open, wondering if Merlin had come with them.

"I am here; you may close the door now." It was as if the mage had read Carter's mind. Merlin appeared in the corner next to the bed. He pushed on the mattress with his hand. "Hmm...comfortable beds. That's one thing we never had in Arthur's day." He sat down and sighed. "Is there one for me?"

Carter nodded. "There are two in my room. You're welcome to sleep there." It occurred to the boy that this guest might be around for quite some time. Maybe he could help him at school with the bullies.... Merlin whispering answers in his ear on tests...that would be helpful.

"I will not," Merlin said adamantly. "You must learn your own answers."

The boy started, astonished. "How—how did you do that? Did you read my mind?"

"Only when it's that loud, young man. I try to avoid reading other people's minds. So much clutter, so many things I would rather not know...but at times thoughts are so strong that they come through whether or not I want to hear them."

"Really, Carter. Thinking about how Merlin can help you? Don't you think he has his own life to worry about?" Penny emptied her backpack into a drawer.

Carter remembered his present situation. "You're right. Besides, we've got something else to deal with. What do you think my great uncle Mortimer came here for?"

"That dude's your great uncle?" She sat on the bed next to Merlin. "Aunt Belinda's brother?"

The boy nodded. "Yup."

"And he came for something...something that belonged to her." She looked from Merlin to Carter. "The door, right?"

"Yup, the door."

"And what did you tell him?"

Carter shrugged. "There are lots of doors around here."

"Good. Evasive answers work really well," Penny commented, most likely from experience.

"For now, but we've got to fix it somehow."

Merlin had risen and walked over to the bookcase. He picked up a book and turned the pages, a delighted expression on his face.

Penny watched him absently for a moment, turning the possibilities over in her mind. "Hmm...my dad has some wood glue in the garage. We could try that."

"Sounds good," Carter responded hopefully.

"Merlin, we're going over to my house. Do you want to come, invisible of course, or would you rather stay here?"

The enchanter, his eyes still on the book, waved them away.

* * * * *

Penny was right. Her dad had two kinds of wood glue sitting on the shelf. The girl grabbed both bottles. "This way we've got two chances," she observed, hurrying out of the garage with Carter at her heels.

Back at Belinda's house they avoided Mrs. Blume and ran up the stairs to Penny's room. Carter hesitated. "Uh, shouldn't we knock or something?"

"Yeah, the invisible magician might be dressing!" Penny snorted. Becoming serious she nodded. "Right. He might not be invisible in there." She knocked politely. There was no answer. She knocked a little harder and put her ear close to the door to hear any response. Nothing.

"Where would he be?" Carter's face took on an anxious expression.

Penny shrugged. "Maybe in the bathroom." She turned the knob and walked in, scanning the room. The boy followed. "Merlin? " Penny called. "Hey, are you in here?"

"What are we going to do?"

"Guess we'll go glue that door," Penny answered in her usual practical voice.

"But what about Merlin?"

"Probably out exploring. He's a big boy. I'm sure he'll turn up when he wants to."

Carter relaxed at her words. "Yeah, guess you're right."

"C'mon. Let's get to work." Penny walked out of the room. With a last glance around him, Carter went after her, silently hoping Merlin would catch up with them. *I never showed him the bathroom,* he thought suddenly. *Oh, well. He could figure it out. Merlin was really old—old enough to take care of those sorts of things.*

* * * * *

The basement didn't seem as scary as it had the first time they were there. The halves of the old door still lay where they had fallen. Penny gazed at them for a moment. "Hmm...I guess we

41

should just glue it right here." She grabbed the statue of the satyr but it was too heavy to lift. "Hey, give me a hand with this."

"Sure." Carter grasped the base and together they were able to pick it up and carry it off to a corner. He grunted as he set his end down on the floor. "That's heavy."

Penny nodded and brushed her hands off on her jeans. "Okay, now we need to see if we can get those broken pieces to go together."

They slid one half into place next to its mate. Penny sighted along the crack as they worked the pieces together until they seemed to fit. "Yeah, I think it will work." They pulled them apart again. "I saw some boards over in that corner." She pointed. "We can slide them under the pieces so we don't glue the thing to your aunt's floor."

They carried the boards back and put them under the door. Penny applied a strip of glue to each side of the break. "Okay, let's put 'em together."

But when they pushed the pieces into place glue squeezed out in a thick, beige stripe.

"I'll get some paper towels," Carter offered. His companion nodded.

"Hurry," she said.

Carter made sure his mother was not in the kitchen before he stepped in and unrolled about a dozen paper towels. He hoped that would be enough. He hurried down the stairs and through the now-familiar stacks of antiques, knowing the glue might dry before they could wipe it all up.

But it was still quite wet when he returned. He handed Penny half of the strip of towels and they carefully wiped the excess glue off the door. Finally they stood back and admired their work. "That just might do it." Penny squished her towels into a ball.

"Guess so," Carter began.

"You really think that will work?" Merlin's voice startled them both.

Penny looked irritated as the enchanter materialized before them. "Ya' know, it's not nice to scare people like that."

"Of course, you are right. I am sorry that I frightened you." Merlin stroked his beard, trying to look serious. He gazed at the repair job. "So, that's your solution."

"Yeah," the girl answered with a shrug.

"Well, it'll look better when the glue dries." Carter gazed at the door, wishing the glue would dry faster.

Penny glanced at the magician. An interesting thought occurred to her. "Unless..." She let the word dangle in the air.

A smile spread across Merlin's face. He nodded and reached into his robe, drawing out a blue crystal sphere. Holding it out on his palm, he closed his eyes a moment. The sphere seemed to come to life with an electric blue light. It brightened the room around them and made Merlin's hair and beard shine with a blue tint.

The children looked on with mouths open as Merlin stooped over the door and ran the globe above the line of glue. Before their astonished eyes the door seemed to grow back together without a trace of damage, or of the hasty repair job. When the enchanter straightened up with a satisfied glance at his handiwork, Penny found her voice. "How did you do that?"

"I'm a mage. How do you think?"

The girl shook her head. "What's with that sphere? Magicians are supposed to use wands."

"So the legends may say." Merlin gazed into the glowing ball. "This," he added as he slowly turned the ball with his slender fingers, "is an ancient tool."

Carter found himself reaching out to touch the sphere. For some reason he was not afraid. The enchanter opened his hand and lowered the ball so the boy could reach it. His hand was still a few inches away but suddenly the ball seemed to jump into it. Carter gasped but still felt no fear, only wonder as he held the sphere up to look into its blue depths.

"Why did it do that?" he asked in a whisper.

Merlin smiled. "It didn't do that. You did."

CHAPTER SEVEN
Shadows

Carter didn't know what to make of the enchanter's words. "What did I do?"

Merlin opened his mouth to answer but shut it quickly when he noticed the suddenly startled look on Carter's face. He turned and followed the boy's gaze in time to catch a glimpse of a shadow that flitted across the floor.

"I—I saw that down here before," the boy whispered. Merlin raised a finger to his lips and shook his head slightly. Carter gulped. He searched in vain for the shadow. Penny stood at his side, scanning the basement. She had seen it, too, this time.

The enchanter raised the blue sphere over his head. Light poured out of it in blue, white and gold streams. The basement seemed to swirl in the brilliant colors. "Come out," Merlin commanded.

The children had to shield their eyes with their hands. They tried to peer out from under their fingers to see if the shadow would come out of hiding. But they could see nothing except Merlin and the great light that shone from his hand.

"It's gone," Merlin muttered, lowering his arm. The light faded quickly and the three stood in the comparatively dim light from the bulbs. Stunned, Penny and Carter stared at the old man. Before either of them could speak they heard the basement door open and Mrs. Blume's voice call out to them. "Carter? Penny? Are you down there?"

Carter gasped but couldn't find his voice. Penny answered, "Yes, Mrs. Blume. We're just looking around a bit."

"Could you come up?" Carter's mom asked, a tremor in her tones. "I...I think I saw someone out in the yard."

Merlin nodded to the children and motioned for them to hurry upstairs.

Carter seemed a little out of breath when he reached the top of the steps behind his faster friend. "Who'd you see, Mom?"

Mrs. Blume shook her head. "It just looked like a shadow. Maybe it's a neighbor kid cutting through the yard, but..." She trailed off, the uncertainty hanging in the air like a wisp of smoke. "I'll show you." She walked into the den and pointed out the window. In the dark room they could see the yard clearly in the light of an almost full moon. The children stared around the yard, noses pressed against the glass.

"I don't see anything," Penny finally offered.

"Probably just a kid," Mrs. Blume murmured.

Carter nodded. "Yeah, just a kid," he repeated, unconvinced.

Penny stepped back from the window. "Got a flashlight? Let's go take a look."

The night had grown chilly. Overhead the stars gleamed in a deep velvet blue sky. Carter followed Penny as she ran ahead to the spot where Mrs. Blume had seen the shadowy figure. He snapped on his flashlight, the light running before him along the cold ground. Penny's light traced the bushes on the edge of the yard. The girl stopped and pointed the light at her feet. "There!" she shouted triumphantly. "Footprints, look!" she called out to Carter's mother as she panted up to join the children.

"What did you find?" Mrs. Blume asked, out of breath.

"Dress shoe prints, big ones," Penny commented. The footprints looked like those of a tall man. They were smooth in the patch of damp earth, as though the man had been wearing business shoes.

"He stood here for a moment, then..." Penny followed the prints behind the tall hedge. "Then he ran along here and into that empty lot next door."

"Maybe I should call the police." Mrs. Blume hesitated, looking from the prints to the house. "Why would he have been looking at that part of the house?"

Carter stared in the direction the intruder would have looked from that spot. All he could see was the stairwell that came up from the basement. Was this the shadow they had seen with Merlin? And was it still lurking around the area?

Suddenly an owl hooted nearby. The three jumped almost visibly from the ground. "What?" the boy asked in a startled tone.

"Just an owl," Penny answered, pointing to the thickest part if the woods. In the dim light they could just make out the figure of a great horned owl sitting on a tree limb. It spread its huge wings and flapped them with slow, noiseless strokes, as if it were in no hurry to leave. The creature circled over Aunt B's house then flew out of sight, still in that unhurried manner.

*   *   *   *   *

Up in Carter's room he and Penny watched the television without speaking. Merlin appeared completely absorbed in the late news. Occasionally he rocked in the big wooden rocker. The kids sat on the bed, more interested in the reactions of their guest than the actual news. "Very good," the enchanter nodded thoughtfully. "As it has always been in our world, what was once thought of as magic is now technology." He frowned as a story about a soccer riot aired.

"Oh, geez!" Penny sighed.

"But the world has not become much better if these violent images are true."

Carter and Penny exchanged an almost embarrassed glance. "There are more people around," the boy commented. "Some things are better but some things..." He trailed off as fans stormed the soccer field, punching and kicking the fans of the other team.

"Why are these people fighting?" Merlin stepped closer to the screen. "Is it an invasion?"

"No." Carter's voice lowered to a hoarse whisper. "They're mad because their team didn't win the game."

The enchanter nodded slowly, still watching the riot. "Well," he added hopefully, "at least they aren't killing each other and taking the heads like the Celtic warriors of old."

"Yeah, that's an improvement," Penny agreed.

Merlin settled back in the rocking chair. "You shouldn't be embarrassed that humans have not all progressed beyond barbarism. That will take a long time." He stroked his beard and nodded, murmuring to himself, "yes, a long, long time." He gave the children a warm smile. "Now, tell me more about your world."

Penny and Carter talked almost all night, telling their guest everything they could think of about modern life. Merlin listened intently, his eyes moving from the children to the objects around the room. It was not until the dawn light began to filter in under and around the edges of the shade that the magician stood and stretched. "I'm afraid I have allowed you to stay up all night. Have you chores to do this morning or may you—what is it you say—sleep in?"

"Oh, we can sleep for a few hours before my mom wants me up to help her out," Carter replied. He yawned.

"Then you both must sleep." The enchanter gestured gracefully with his long fingers.

"Oh, I don't feel..." Penny paused to yawn, "at all tired." And suddenly she slumped in the chair, asleep. Carter, too, dropped into a deep slumber on the bed.

Merlin rose, gazing fondly at the two. "Rest well, my dears." He picked up Penny and carried her to the next room, as easily as if she were a small child. He laid her on the bed. She stirred when he placed the covers over her. As he reached for the door he disappeared from sight. The door closed softly behind him.

* * * * *

"Carter! Penny!" Mrs. Blume called from the bottom of the stairs. The boy awoke, startled. He glanced quickly around the room. The clock read 10:20. His first thought was, "Where is Merlin?"

"Coming, Mom," he called back, hoping his guest was somewhere nearby and invisible.

He heard a knock on the door. "Hey, sleepyhead, c'mon!" Penny 's voice rang cheerfully in the hall. Carter threw back the covers and hurried to the door. He opened it enough to peer out at his friend.

"You two decent?" Penny glanced over Carter's head to see if Merlin was there.

"Uh, I don't know." He looked behind him for a trace of the enchanter's presence.

47

"I'll let you know."

The girl gave him a quizzical look, and then nodded. "Okay. I'll go down and help your mom with breakfast." She turned and tripped down the steps, calling out a "Good morning" to Mrs. Blume.

Back in the bedroom Carter whispered, "Merlin? Are you here?" He waited for an answer but none came. "Where did you go?" he asked the air around him. Finally he decided that he was alone and began to change his clothes. He noticed how hungry he really felt as he hurried down the stairs to the kitchen.

Mrs. Blume spooned a large helping of scrambled eggs onto her son's plate. "Mmm...these smell great!" Carter grabbed his fork and scooped up a mouthful of the fluffy, yellow concoction. He ate with good appetite, oblivious, for the moment, to any care.

Suddenly he got a kick under the table. Penny gave him a meaningful glance. "Well?" she mouthed.

"What?" he shot back in silence.

Penny glanced at Mrs. Blume, who had turned to the sink and had begun scrubbing the frying pan under the faucet. The girl kicked Carter again. "Merlin!" she almost muttered out loud.

"Ow!" the boy yowled.

Mrs. Blume half turned to look at the two children. "What on earth is going on?"

"Uh...uh," Carter stumbled over his words. "I...uh...bit my lip, Mom. Nothing serious." As soon as his mother turned back to the sink the boy glared at Penny. She glared back just as fiercely. Carter shrugged to tell her he didn't know where Merlin was. The girl shook her head, the red curls bouncing around her shoulders. Then she picked up her fork and settled down to eat her eggs.

When they finished eating the two picked up their plates with one accord and brought them to the sink. With a gallant gesture Carter insisted that Penny rinse her plate first. As he stepped up to the faucet for his turn, the doorbell rang.

"I hope it's not those weird antique dealers again," Mrs. Blume groaned as she walked down the hall to the door. "Oh, Uncle Mort. How are you this morning?" Penny and Carter exchanged meaningful glances. Without a word the two drifted nonchalantly down the hall and into the parlor where Uncle Mort stood, hands clasped in front of him as if he were cold. He spoke in apologetic tones to Mrs. Blume.

"Really, I do hate to bother you about it at this time, knowing how busy you are with estate matters..."

"Well, I do wonder why Aunt B didn't make you executor, since you are her brother." She hesitated. "I'm sorry, I hope I haven't..."

Mort shook his head with a dreary smile. "No, that is quite all right, my dear. I think my sister feared that I might be...uh...inaccessible in case of her demise." He waved the uncomfortable moment away with a flutter of his pale hand. "I am glad she chose you, Clarice. You have such a good head for business. I would be utterly lost in all this legalese."

His black eyes spied the children hovering in the foyer. "Good morning, children."

Carter waved a little guiltily. "Hi, Uncle Mort."

"And who is this lovely young lady with you, nephew?"

"Penny. She lives behind us in the white house," Carter answered, feeling a little awkward.

"Very nice to meet you." Mortimer extended his hand to Penny, who stepped forward to grasp it firmly in her own. "I'm Mortimer Feltree, young miss..." He let the silence dangle, waiting for her answer.

"Oh, Morgan, Penny Morgan." His handshake felt weak to the girl. "Nice to meet you, too." She stepped back as a strange feeling came over her. She glanced from Uncle Mort to Carter. The feeling was not unpleasant but the girl wondered what it meant.

"Where is this box of yours, anyway?" Mrs. Blume asked her uncle.

Mort turned back to his niece. "Downstairs, in the basement, I believe."

Penny elbowed her friend as the adults made their way past them and toward the basement door. "Look," she whispered in Carter's ear.

"What?"

"His shoes." She pointed to the strange man's feet. He wore dress shoes, dulled by what looked like smeared mud. Carter's eyes went wide. Penny held a warning finger to her lips as he opened his mouth to speak. She shook her head and gestured for the boy to follow her. He nodded and fell in line behind his friend.

Down in the basement Mrs. Blume gestured around her with a sigh. "Look at all this stuff. You can understand why I haven't been able to find that door. I have so much to go through and I've only just started."

"Of course," Mortimer replied with a sympathetic tone. "Now that I have returned I would be happy to help you out. After all, Belinda was my own sister." He flashed a spare smile, which looked more disturbing than reassuring to the children, who hovered almost protectively at Mrs. Blume's elbow.

Carter gave Penny a look that clearly said, "I bet he would like to 'help out'." The girl nodded.

"Well, look around, Uncle Mortimer. I really don't know where your box would be down in this mess."

"That's fine, Clarice." Mortimer moved toward a large, mahogany wardrobe that towered in a corner. "If Belinda didn't move it I should find it over here." He opened the doors and rummaged around inside.

Penny and Carter inched closer to get a better view.

"Ah, here it is." Mortimer pulled a carved, black box from a shelf inside the wardrobe.

Mrs. Blume stepped closer to take a look. "Oh!" she exclaimed. "What a lovely box!" She reached out to touch it. Mortimer held it closer.

"It...uh...needs some restoration work, Clarice."

Mrs. Blume withdrew her hand. Even in the dim light from the bulb Carter could see his mother blush. Mortimer, meanwhile, had covered the box in a thick, black cloth he had taken from his pocket.

Still holding his burden close, he turned to take a look at the rest of the basement. "Mind if I look around?"

Mrs. Blume shook her head. "Please do. You probably know most of this stuff better than I do."

Mortimer flashed that thin smile again. "Perhaps you are right, my dear." He set off through the maze of antiques, Penny and Carter close behind. Mrs. Blume lagged in the rear, gazing at the vast array of objects.

The spare figure stopped in front of the door that Merlin had magically repaired. Hands on hips he stared at it, a bemused expression on his face. Mrs. Blume moved to her uncle's side. "Is that the one?" she asked.

He nodded. "Yes, the very same. Very ancient, this door."

"What time period?"

"It dates from the middle ages, Clarice." He reached out and ran his long fingers down the exact line where the door had broken. Carter caught his breath. Penny elbowed him, hoping Uncle Mort had not heard the boy's barely audible gasp.

"Very valuable," Mortimer continued. "Priceless, perhaps." He shook his head. "At least it once was."

"So it has dropped in value?" Mrs. Blume asked.

Her uncle nodded. "Yes."

"I don't understand how the antiques market works. Will it go up in value again?"

"Perhaps, Clarice. Perhaps it will." He stroked his chin while the children exchanged glances. How would the door go up in value again? Would he try to trap Merlin in it again?

There was no time to ponder. The chimes of the doorbell broke the momentary silence. "I wonder who that could be?" Mrs. Blume excused herself and hurried up the stairs. Penny moved over to Mortimer. From the glance she gave Carter the boy understood that they shouldn't trust his great uncle alone in the basement.

"So," Penny began. "Where did that box come from? Is it old?"

"Oh, yes. Very old." Mortimer turned and started toward the stairs, the box tucked protectively under his arm. He hurried up the steps and into the kitchen, Penny following close behind him, trying to get a better look at the box. She heard Carter panting a few steps back as she stepped through the doorway.

Mortimer slowed his pace as he entered the hall. He stopped in the shadow of the mahogany grandfather clock. Penny watched him carefully as he cocked his head to listen to the conversation in the parlor. Carter elbowed his friend.

"That's the weird old woman who was here yesterday," he whispered.

The girl nodded, a quizzical look crossing her freckled face. Why was she back again?

They heard the woman's honey tones. "I can make it very much worth your while."

"Well, even if you could," answered an exasperated Mrs. Blume, "I still have to carry out my aunt's wishes and it seems that she, apparently, wanted my uncle to have the door. In fact, I don't know why I even let you in this house!"

"Why, I am so sorry to bother you, my dear, I had no idea that your uncle was...still alive."

"Alive? Well, he's been away..." Mrs. Blume trailed off in confusion. "You know my uncle?"

"Why, yes. Of course, he may not know me since I have never met him personally. He is well known in...the antique circles." The voice oiled its way around its target, probing for further information. "Have you seen him?"

At this Mortimer cursed under his breath. He glanced back at the children, as if to let them know he had been well aware of their presence, then strode quickly down the hall and into the parlor. Carter and Penny followed partway, hiding in the shadows so they could see what transpired next.

"Miss Nimway, what a surprise to see you here." Mortimer's voice barely hid the displeasure he obviously felt at seeing the unwelcome guest.

The elderly woman ignored the slight and greeted him in the same honeyed tones she had used on Mrs. Blume. "Mortimer Feltree, I had no idea you were..." she paused, "in the country."

"How would you, since my sister never spoke to you after her travels in Europe?" He waved his hand as if to dismiss the subject. "However, that is of no importance now. She has passed on and left her estate in the capable hands of her niece." He inclined his head toward Clarice.

Miss Nimway glanced with calculating eyes from him to the confused Mrs. Blume. She nodded and smiled a stiff, polite little smile. "Why yes, of course you are correct. I hope she will consider selling the door to me."

"Well," Mrs. Blume interposed. "I simply cannot sell you the door. As I already told you, it belongs to my uncle now."

The old woman nodded again in acquiescence. "Yes. You did tell me that. Then," she continued on another tack, turning her gaze full upon Mortimer. "Perhaps you will sell it to me." Their eyes locked. Mortimer appeared transfixed.

Carter whispered in Penny's ear. "What is she doing to him?" The girl shrugged.

Merlin's voice popped into both the children's minds. There was no sound. "She is trying to mesmerize him," he said. The two started. "Stay calm," Merlin warned. "Don't be afraid. I'm simply using telepathy." They nodded and turned back to the drama unfolding in the parlor.

Mortimer and the elderly woman remained as before, locked in an invisible battle that only they could understand. Mrs. Blume, upset by the intensity of the moment, broke the silence. "I'm sure my uncle is still upset by the loss of his sister. I have to ask you to leave now."

Miss Nimway nodded slowly, her eyes still fixed on Mortimer's. Then she dropped her gaze to the box in the crook of his arm. Part of the covering cloth had fallen away from one side. A slight smile shivered across her lips and disappeared into a polite mask. "Now that is an unusual box. Late Victorian?"

"No, much older than that," Mortimer answered quickly.

"But it seems to be in very good condition. A skilled craftsman must have restored that for you."

"It is my work." The old woman glanced at Mortimer's face and smiled in satisfaction as her flattery soothed the strained creases around his eyes.

Mortimer inhaled sharply and made a slight bow. "I must be going now. I wish you a good day." With that he turned quickly and strode down the hall to the kitchen.

Miss Nimway stared after him, a light smile lifting the corners of her lips. "So good to have finally met you, Mr. Feltree." She nodded to Mrs. Blume. "Thank you, my dear Clarice. We have taken enough of your time." She took her companion's arm. "Come, we have much to do."

The gentleman nodded to Clarice. "Thank you. Good day." They stepped lightly through the door and down the walk.

Mrs. Blume lost no time shutting the door after them. She leaned back on the panel and sighed. Catching sight of the children she addressed them. "I'm not sure I know what that was all about." Carter shrugged his shoulders, trying to look nonchalant. "Maybe

Uncle Mort knows," his mother murmured to no one in particular. She straightened and walked down the hall.

Apparently Mortimer had left, leaving the kitchen door ajar. The children pushed their way out the door at the same time, trying to catch a glimpse of him but he had disappeared. They stood in the yard looking around at the bushes as though he might have taken refuge behind one of them. Penny put her hands on her hips and gave a low whistle. "That was fast. How did he do that?"

CHAPTER EIGHT
Faerie Blood

Penny's house stood almost exactly opposite Aunt Belinda's strange mansion, just outside the four acres of woods that comprised the old woman's back yard. The Morgan's house had been built in the open and inviting style of a country farmhouse. Inside the walls looked bright as though Penny's mother had just scrubbed them. The furniture would have turned their neighbor's nose up because every piece was modern with bright flowered prints.

Carter liked this house a lot better than his aunt's. For one thing, he could sit anywhere without getting a disapproving stare. "Make yourself at home," Mrs. Morgan would say. And he believed she meant it.

As they ran up the stairs to Penny's room her mother called out a cheery hello to Carter. He waved his hand behind him and called back, "Hi, Mrs. Morgan."

"How's your mom?"

He stopped and turned to look down into the woman's smiling face. It looked as fresh and bright as her home. He smiled back. "She's fine. Just kind of busy with the estate."

Mrs. Morgan nodded. "Of course. I'll have to go over with an apple pie. I know she likes my pies." She gave him a wink. "And I think you might like them almost as much as your mom."

The boy grinned. "Yep!" He had fond memories of those pies, with their lightly firm slices of tart apple and sweet cinnamon inside. Even the flaky crusts tasted good, not at all like some pies with their tasteless, cardboard-like crusts. He would cut those kinds

55

of crust off the pie and leave it on the plate, whenever he could get away with it.

Up in Penny's spacious room he flopped onto a blue beanbag chair. As he felt himself sucked into its shapeless depths he sighed, glad to be away from the oppressive atmosphere that permeated and choked every corner of his great aunt's house.

Penny shut the door and turned excitedly, looking for Merlin. He flashed into view as he started to sink into his own beanbag chair. "These are strange...handy, but very strange." He grinned. Despite the long, white beard, his face took on a decidedly boyish look.

"Merlin," Penny began. "Why do those antique dealers want your door?"

The enchanter shifted in the chair and stroked his beard thoughtfully. "Probably, because, they are the ones that put me there in the first place."

Carter caught his breath. "Them? But...but that was so long ago...wasn't it?"

"Oh, indeed, young sir. A very long time ago." He paused, eyeing the two children as though deciding whether or not to take them into his confidence. "But not long for those of almost pure faerie blood."

Penny and Carter looked at him in surprise and amazement. "Faerie blood?" they asked in unison.

"I thought faeries were those wispy-looking creatures, with— with wings and all," the boy stammered.

"Oh, some of them are, but they come in all shapes and sizes...and powers." He took a deep breath. "What I am about to tell you is something that very few people like yourself know. That woman is really Nimue, a tree spirit from a forest in England. Her partner is an old apprentice of mine, a man whose mother was also a tree spirit."

Penny looked skeptical. "But a tree spirit...I mean, how could a creature like that trap you, and transform into that...that nasty woman? Do...uh...tree spirits have that kind of power? "

Merlin stared at the ceiling. "No, not usually. But the females do have, besides their powers over trees, certain...um…powers, no, influences over men."

"Then the stories," Carter began excitedly, "the ones I've read about you being bewitched by Nimue—they're true?"

The children stared as the enchanter's face blushed a bright red. They could even see it under his whiskers. "Yes," he answered quietly. "Of course, it depends upon which one you read..."

Merlin stood and faced them. "I was an old man. I saw that I could no longer help Arthur. He had chosen his way and would not change it...or listen to his old teacher anymore. I grieved a long time after he died, in a battle he should never have fought." He sighed. "Nimue came to me saying she sought wisdom from a great mage, me. How I could have been so deceived, so foolishly flattered by such a woman, such a beautiful woman? It could only have happened because I was at a very weak point in my life. At another time, in my days of teaching Arthur, I would never have fallen into her trap."

"What wisdom was she looking for, then?" Penny asked, enthralled by the story.

"She claimed she wished to help mankind and so wanted to learn to use her faerie powers for good, to possibly help bring peace before the country was torn apart by war."

"So," Carter interjected, "that was the way she sucked you in, so she could learn more magic from you."

"Yes, at first." The old man shook his head, his beard trailing back and forth across his chest. "Then, she seemed interested in me. She said she loved being around me and I...I longed to be with her. I really think I fell in love with her."

Silence filled the room. Finally Penny murmured: "I'm sorry."

Carter swallowed hard. "Uh, these faerie powers... What are they? Who has them?"

Merlin stopped, a half-smile playing over his aged features. "In ancient days, days long gone by and forgotten by most of the human race, there lived a wise and very advanced people." The enchanter's eyes took on a brighter, more youthful light.

"And in those enlightened times the faerie folk lived openly upon the earth, without fear of humans. They allowed themselves to be known in their true forms. Many were tiny and delicate with wings, just as you have them in your faerie tales. Others were tall and graceful; they tended to the plants and animals, as well as people, in need. Some devoted themselves to the forests as tree spirits, others lived within the waters of streams, lakes, rivers, and such."

He sat down in the rocker and moved back and forth in silence for a few moments, lost in what must have been a beautiful memory. The smile changed, sometimes growing, sometimes disappearing altogether, as the story moved in his mind.

Penny shifted her position on the bed. She coughed politely to let Merlin know that they were still waiting for more of the story. He looked up, almost startled, then grinned.

"Ah, yes, I was still trying to answer the young master's question." Now he rocked more slowly. "Yes, those were lovely, tremendous times, with humans and faerie peoples living in cooperation and helping each other whenever needed. It was not at all unusual for faeries and humans to fall in love and marry, and, of course, have families. And so the faerie blood and faerie powers entered the human race everywhere. Eventually every human born had at least a little of the ancient faerie blood in them."

"Uh...does that mean..." Carter trailed off, almost afraid to ask the obvious.

Merlin nodded thoughtfully. "Yes, it means that everyone has faerie blood in them, even you, young man."

The children looked stunned. "All of us?" the two asked in unison.

"Yes."

There was a pause. Finally Carter shook his head. "Well, it hasn't done me any good."

"Not so," Merlin replied. "All of us share the faerie blood, some have more than others but we all share in its powers."

"Well, I don't have any power or else the bullies at school wouldn't come after me so much." The boy hung his head and sighed.

The old enchanter looked with compassion on Carter as the boy, with shoulders drooped, struggled to hold back the tears that suddenly welled in his eyes. He wiped them away, almost angrily with his sleeve. "That's a nice story, Merlin, but I don't believe I have any special power. I can't seem to do anything right."

"That's not true!" Penny cried. "Don't you even remember how well you did in Little League last summer? You were the best player your team ever had!"

"Well, maybe I can do one thing right." The boy raised his head, pride gleaming in his clear brown eyes.

Merlin smiled. "What is this thing, this Little League?"

"It's baseball played by kids on lots of teams," Penny began, before launching into a passionate explanation of the great American pastime. Merlin's eyes widened with interest at the idea of this well-loved game.

"So, Carter is good at this, then?"

"Good? He's incredible! His team made it into the playoffs. My mom took me to see them play." Penny's voice rose in excitement. "I saw him catch fly balls that even professional ballplayers would have trouble getting. They just seemed to fly right into his glove. And, boy! Could he throw them back to base! His teammates hardly had to reach out to catch them! And you should have seen him at bat. Every time he swung at the ball it was a home run, and the pitchers got so scared of him that they wouldn't throw anything near the plate. "

Carter sat grinning and blushing through Penny's praise. His back had straightened, and he had raised his head with pride at his accomplishments—and Penny's admiration.

Merlin knitted his eyebrows together. "And who taught you to do these things?"

"Ever since I could walk my mom started playing catch with me." He closed his eyes for a moment in thought then continued with enthusiasm. "Mom was great at every sport. In college she was voted most valuable player in softball, field hockey and basketball."

"Ah," Merlin responded. "Then it runs in the family."

"You mean sports?"

"No, young man. I mean your gift." The enchanter stroked his beard. "So, how is your mother related to Belinda?"

"Uh, she's the daughter of B's younger sister, Marguerite, my grandma." He paused. "We never knew what happened to her or grandpa. We wrote and called, and finally drove up to their house. She and grandpa were gone. I hardly remember them now, it's been so long since I last saw them."

"I'm sorry to hear that. Your grandfather...what was his name?" Merlin asked.

"Griffin, uh...Michael Griffin," Carter said the last triumphantly, pleased that he had remembered.

Merlin said nothing but his face became more thoughtful than before. Slowly he nodded and rose from the chair. He crossed the room, became invisible and opened the door without a word.

Carter sat, stunned, wondering what was happening in the enchanter's mind. Did he know what might have happened to his grandparents? "Wait, Merlin. Where are you going? Do you have any idea where my grandparents went?"

The door shut. "I hope to discover the answer to that last question by searching the rooms in your great aunt's house."

"Oh," Carter responded in a quiet voice. He stood up reluctantly, ready but not anxious for action.

"Now," Merlin began, appearing again. "I am sure such curious young people as yourselves would likely have explored Belinda's house."

"Well, a lot of it, anyway," Penny piped up. She didn't go on to say that Carter had been too afraid to explore all the halls they had found in the strange mansion—halls that seemed that they might go on forever.

"Then it would be most logical if you would lead the way." He smiled and disappeared. The door opened wide. "After you," Merlin said in his most gallant voice.

The children each stepped through the door and waited for the invisible enchanter to exit the room and close the door behind him. "C'mon," Penny whispered as she started down the steps.

CHAPTER NINE
The Chamber of Art

Mrs. Blume must have been off in one of the farther rooms, since the car sat in the driveway and Carter heard no answers to his calls for his mother. "I guess the coast is clear for now," he whispered to his companions.

Penny strode boldly past the wide staircase and turned down a long hallway. Carter hurried after her, glancing around to make sure Merlin stayed invisible. Several doors stood half-open along the corridor. They stopped and peered into each room. Most contained collections of antiques of various eras and styles. One room was filled with dark Victorian armoires, another with tall, canopied beds. "She sure did love to collect, didn't she," Penny commented as they looked in one room filled with gramophones and victrolas. Two of the walls had glass-enclosed shelves entirely crammed with wax cylinders and old records.

At the end of the hall they had the choice of an ample, well-lit passage on the left and a smaller, darker, corridor on the right. Carter shivered and pointed to the left. "Let's go that way."

Penny shook her head. Merlin appeared beside her, studying her face. "And which way draws you, young lady?"

The girl turned to the right and took a step into the dark hall. "Yes," she said in a subdued voice. "This is the way."

"How do you know that?" Carter asked. "We've never gone this way before."

"I...I feel it." She paused, thinking. "No, not just that...I see it somehow, in my mind."

Merlin nodded. "Then that is the way we shall go." With that he turned down the right hall and strode ahead. Penny followed the enchanter.

Carter hesitated then trotted up to join them. He could barely see but he was afraid to touch the wall to guide himself along. Instead, he ended up running into it. "Ow!" he exclaimed as he fell to the floor.

The other two stopped. "What happened? " Penny asked in a whisper.

"I can't see, so I ran into the wall!" Carter struggled to his feet, alternately rubbing his left shoulder and both knees, which had all banged the wall or the floor.

Merlin stepped to the boy's side and touched him gently on the top of the head. "Are you hurt?" Carter nodded. "Perhaps I can help with that. Just relax for a moment."

"Okay." The boy felt a little confused. How could Merlin help with the pain? He did his best to relax. The enchanter placed his hands on Carter's shoulders. Soon, a comforting feeling of warmth began to fill his body. He felt far away from the scary hall. In fact he felt removed from everything except the wonderful warmth.

Merlin removed his hands but the feeling of warmth remained in the boy's shoulder and knees. "How do you feel now?" Merlin asked.

Carter opened his eyes in surprise. "Wow! I don't hurt at all!" He looked up into the enchanter's face in wonder. "How did you do that?"

The old man smiled. "I have learned a thing or two in my lengthy life."

Penny had watched the two closely. "Cool!" was all she could say. And Penny was never at a loss for words.

"Let's go," Merlin said in a quiet but commanding tone. He turned and began down the corridor again.

Penny took Carter's arm to help him but he shook it off. "I'm okay," he muttered. "I just wish I could see!"

"Ah, yes." The enchanter stopped and reached into his robe. "I can help with that." He held up the sphere, which suddenly illuminated the corridor with pure white light.

Carter smiled. "Thanks. That's a whole lot better." Now the hall didn't look so scary to him anymore.

The trio strode down, peering into rooms they found along the way. At another, even smaller hallway, they stopped. Merlin took a few steps in and swept his light as far as it would go. "Young lady. What do you feel from this one?" He turned to gaze at Penny.

She moved into the hall and stopped. "This one feels very strange, different from the other." Taking a few more steps she put her hands up, and then turned to touch the wall. Penny looked back at the others. "I don't like this one at all." She paused and shook her head. "I really don't like the feeling down here. But that is why I know this is the way."

"Very well," Merlin replied. "Then let us proceed." Holding the light high in front of him, he moved down the new corridor a little more slowly than before.

Carter looked from Penny to the enchanter. Now he felt afraid again. He bit back his own protests and followed his friends. He wondered why Merlin was relying on Penny to lead the way. Pondering this subject as he walked, he didn't notice when the girl stopped and grabbed the old man's sleeve. Carter, deep in thought, ran right into Merlin and found himself on the floor once again.

"Can't you ever walk anywhere without falling?" he muttered to himself. He jumped up quickly so no one would have to help him.

"Hmm...Young man, do you bump into things often?" Merlin's eyes twinkled with mischief.

"No...well, maybe...sometimes," the boy responded, confused.

"You okay?" Penny asked.

"Yeah, just a little..."

"Embarrassed?" the old man asked in a soft voice.

"Uh, yeah." Carter could feel the heat in his face as he blushed.

"Don't," the enchanter said. "You are young and your nature will sometimes work against you. That is why those with strong faerie blood are usually never trained until they become adults, no longer at the mercy of the changes in their bodies, or the whirl of contrary thoughts in their minds."

"What?" Penny and Carter both echoed.

Merlin sat down on the floor. The children followed suit. "Well," he began. "The people who demonstrate certain powers generally have more faerie blood in their veins than others. It isn't always so but it is usually that way." He took a deep breath. "After they are grown and have gained in wisdom, the parent or relative in their family who has received training, takes the young man or woman under their wing in order to teach them about their heritage and how to develop their powers further."

Carter's eyes widened. "Do you mean my mom was trained? She doesn't seem magical at all!"

"She should have been offered the opportunity by one of her parents, aunts or uncles. She would only have trained if she wished to do so. There are powerful people who decline this offer." Merlin smiled. "But that is something you should ask your mother, young man."

He turned to Penny. "Now, my dear, tell me what frightened you."

Penny felt better sitting next to the enchanter. She wasn't even sure why she had become scared so suddenly. "I felt the presence of something dangerous and evil. It felt like some horrible monster was coming after us."

Merlin nodded and held up the sphere for her to see. The light dimmed to a very soft blue, like the sky. "Tell me what you see."

The blue felt even more comforting to the girl. Penny watched the sphere. In a few moments the color changed and she was witnessing a scene in a strange room. Lit only by oil lamps and candles, the room drew her and repelled her at the same time. At the center of the room stood a woman robed in black. She was tying something light-colored around a small, flat object. When she had completed this task she held the thing up in triumph. At that point her hood fell back and revealed her features. Penny gasped.

"It's...it's your aunt, Carter!"

"What do you see, my dear," Merlin asked with patience.

"Don't you see it, too, Merlin?"

"No." He smiled. "I see different things."

"Like what?" the girl asked.

"Distant dangers, new hopes," he answered. "Now, tell us."

Penny related the scene in the strange room. "Then I could finally see her face...and it was your great aunt, Belinda."

"My aunt?" Carter stood open-mouthed. For a moment he couldn't find words to respond to Penny's vision.

Merlin put a hand on each of their shoulders. "We must be very close to what we are seeking. These things that you have seen, my child, are from the past. They hang heavy in this hallway."

Carter swallowed hard. "Will we get hurt if we find...whatever it is we're looking for?"

Merlin smiled reassuringly. "I will not allow either of you to be hurt. Belinda is dead and can do nothing to us now. I wish to see if she has left any secrets behind." He turned and, raising the sphere, peered down the hall. The sphere grew more luminous than before. "Let us continue our journey. It is not far now."

For a while they walked in silence, occasionally opening doors along the way. Each of these rooms held antiques from the Renaissance. Most were weapons of war or armor. Once in awhile they saw lush chairs and beds, with beautifully carved tables. Penny opened the next door.

"Wow! This stuff is old!" she exclaimed.

Merlin gazed into the room, a strange expression on his face. Carter wormed his way between them to get a good look, too. "What kind of antiques are those?" he asked, after glancing over the room that contained ancient trunks, chairs, and a couple of tables littered with bags so deteriorated that their contents of brilliant, multicolored gemstones had fallen out of the seams. Antique wood and stone working tools lay rusting on the floor, as if tossed there long ago by an owner who had never returned.

The enchanter stepped back out of the doorway. "Those are from my time."

"Really?" the children responded in unison.

"Yes." Merlin seemed suddenly tired.

Penny moved back into the hall, her eyes on the enchanter. She felt strange as she watched him, almost as though she was sharing his feelings. "Whose were those?" she asked in a quiet voice.

"Mine," the old man answered. "They belonged to me."

Carter stood in the doorway and stared at Merlin. Penny took a step closer and laid a comforting hand on the enchanter's arm. Merlin looked down at her and smiled. "It is strange to see them here, but I have, just recently, learned why. Long ago, the Feltree family took it upon themselves to protect me. So, it is only logical that they would care for my things as well."

The children waited for an explanation while Merlin stroked his beard. He held the sphere at eye level, gazing into its blue and white depths. After a moment he continued his story. "This lovely object has many uses." The two fixed their eyes on the globe as gold and silver sparkles began to swirl slowly from the center. "You both know two of its uses, that of giving light and that of revealing what may come to pass in the future."

He brought the sphere down to chest level. "This wonderful tool can also act as a conduit of recorded history. I have spent most of your sleeping hours learning all that it can tell me about the past fifteen hundred years. This knowledge comes from what you would call a data bank that is kept in a secret place of which I shall speak later."

"Wow! That's so cool!" Penny exclaimed in wonder. Suddenly a new idea occurred to her. "Does that sphere also translate our language for you, because they certainly didn't speak modern English back in the Middle Ages."

Merlin smiled. "You have an astute mind, dear girl." He nodded. "Yes, it does, indeed, translate for me, but it also carries more than enough information so that the bearer may quickly learn an unfamiliar tongue."

Carter cocked his head in interest. "Didn't they speak Old English back then?"

"No, Old English came a bit later. The learned spoke Latin as well as Brythonic."

"Brythonic?" Carter mouthed the strange word.

Before the boy could ask another question, Merlin spoke. "I have gotten off the track, as you would say. We have little time to discuss ancient languages now. Let me return to my explanation of the relationship between the Feltree family and me.

"The Feltrees were a noble family, very loyal to Arthur, and many of them had been my students. When they found out that Nimue had put me under a spell they searched everywhere until they found me." The enchanter nodded his head. "Yes, they were a fine family." He glanced at Carter. "Yes, some of them are noble and loyal to this day."

"But not all of us," the boy added in a low voice.

Merlin simply shrugged. "Some people abuse their powers and some do not. After all, we're still human."

Penny's curiosity got the best of her. "So, then what happened?"

"Then, the family themselves worked together to bring my tree down carefully, so as not to do me further damage. They brought the tree to their castle and the elder Feltree, Linus, tried to free me from the spell but to no avail. Instead, he was able to compress my essence down into a relatively small part of the tree." Merlin smiled. "It was, indeed, quite a large tree.

"Their purpose was to protect and hide me in an everyday object until one of their descendants should be born with the skill to release me from the wood. In fact," and he turned his gaze on Penny, "Linus had a daughter with a gift similar to yours, dear girl. She told the family that she had seen me being released by a Feltree descendant." He patted Carter's shoulder. "What she did not say was that this powerful person would be a boy who was not even trained to perform such a feat."

Carter grinned and blushed. "You mean..." He couldn't believe that he could do something so important in his life. "You mean...uh...me?"

The enchanter nodded. "I do, indeed. I owe you a debt of gratitude."

"But all I did was break the door."

"Yes," Merlin replied. "How many others had tried to release me that way?"

The boy shrugged. "I don't know."

"Exactly," Merlin said. It wasn't really a definite answer but Carter decided he would take it as a compliment.

"So," Penny began, "Carter's great aunt decided she was the one who would get you out?"

"And Great Uncle Mortimer might have been trying to use your door for some evil purpose."

Merlin shook his head. "That is not clear from the record. We have yet to discover their motives for what they may or may not have done." He glanced at the room that still held his belongings. "Close that door. We have not found what we seek here."

Carter shut the door and the trio moved down the hall. After winding further along the passageway, they found themselves in front of a door with strange markings on it. This was a heavier door than the others they had seen, and it had a large padlock near the handle. Obviously the room must have held something of greater value than any other room in the house.

Penny touched the markings on the door. "The snake eating its tail, I've seen that before...and the Celtic knots. What do all these symbols mean?" She pointed at the groups of notched lines. "It looks like some sort of writing."

Merlin gazed at them, holding the sphere aloft. "They are." He read them carefully. "Yes, this is one of the languages of the Ancient Ones, inscribed in the Ogham alphabet." He touched the lock, which suddenly sprang open. He removed it from the door and put it into his robe. Turning to the children the enchanter placed a firm hand on the door and began to open it. "This, apparently, is Belinda's Chamber of Art, the room where powerful magic is often worked. Shall we, as you would say, check it out?"

Penny nodded eagerly. Carter took a deep breath. "Are you sure it's okay to go in there?"

"She's not around any more," Penny observed. "I don't think it matters now."

"Oh." Carter cast around for another reason not to enter the strange room.

The girl took his arm. "C'mon. How bad can it be?" Carter could think of several answers to that question but decided to keep them to himself. As Merlin pushed the door open a heavy scent of incense flowed out into the hall, making Carter choke and cough. Penny waved a hand in front of her. "Whew! Nice smell but too much!"

The enchanter entered the room and looked around quickly to make sure no one was there. The kids stepped in and gazed around in awe. On the walls hung huge old tapestries depicting scenes of various battles. Four silken banners, one yellow, one red, one blue and one green, hung from the top of each wall. On the floor of the chamber someone had carefully painted a large white circle with a red triangle off to one side. In the middle of the circle stood a heavy table covered with a black cloth.

Penny drew closer to the table to peer at the array of candleholders, incense burners, knives, and other items she did not recognize. She gasped as her eyes fell upon a flat object that looked like the one in her vision. "There it is," she whispered, pointing at it with her finger.

Merlin came to stand beside her. "That is what you saw?" The girl nodded. "Well, then, let's have a better look." He bent down to study it, placing his sphere on the table. The object seemed to be made of wood, but some sort of fibers had been wrapped around it, making it difficult to recognize. Merlin placed his hand over it for a moment without touching it.

"What is that stuff wrapped around it?" Penny asked.

"It appears to be spider webbing." Merlin picked up the object and looked at the other side.

Carter moved closer to get a better view. "That looks like a picture frame. Is there a picture inside it?"

Murmuring in a strange language, Merlin suddenly tore the webbing from the frame. A picture of a man and a woman was revealed. "Just as I thought, someone put a spell on this." He lowered the picture so the children could see it better. "Do either of you know who these people are?"

Penny shook her head. Carter stared at the picture, barely able to take his eyes away from it. "I know," he said slowly. "Those are my grandparents."

Merlin gazed at the couple in the picture. They seemed to have just entered their midyears, with not a strand of gray in their hair. They looked peaceful and very healthy. Wisdom and patience shone in their eyes. "So this must be Marguerite Feltree. A lovely woman, I might add. Hmm...Michael Griffin, yes, he comes from an old family as well. I knew an ancestor of his."

"Did, uh..." Carter swallowed and tried again. "Did my great aunt kill them?"

Merlin smiled slightly. He turned to Carter. "I have good news for you, young man. Your grandparents are not dead, just away for a long time."

"What was the spell?" Penny asked.

"Only something to keep them from returning home from wherever they went. They have not been harmed." He brushed the last of the dust and webbing from the picture. "And now the spell is completely broken." He handed the picture to Carter, who hesitated at first, and then took it very carefully into his hands. "This is yours, my boy."

Carter looked with wonder from Merlin to the picture. "Thanks." He was about to ask why his great aunt didn't want his grandparents to return when the enchanter raised a hand, motioning them to silence.

"Someone comes," he whispered.

CHAPTER TEN
Mortimer's Work

The children froze. Now they could hear the soft steps coming down the hall. Merlin snatched up the sphere and glanced around for a hiding place. He pointed to a tapestry in a corner. The children headed for it in silence. They could see the tapestry moving gently back and forth as if it were in a slight breeze. The enchanter pulled it back, revealing a doorway that stopped a few feet away at a brick wall. Merlin gestured for the children to enter. They hurried in as the tapestry fell back into place and the light from the sphere went out.

The steps slowed as they approached the room. Light from a powerful flashlight gleamed through the crack at the bottom of the door. Carter moved back a little, stepping on someone's foot. He was about to cry out in surprise when a strong but invisible hand covered his mouth. Merlin! He hadn't seen him enter the doorway with them.

Now the sound of the steps had stopped. Penny looked over at Carter. He seemed a bit frightened as he glanced from her to the small opening between the tapestry and the doorway. She touched his shoulder and gave him a little smile. The boy returned it with a hesitant one of his own, and then took a deep breath.

The door creaked slightly as someone opened it. The beam of the flashlight painted each wall in turn, pausing at the tapestry then completing its circuit. Finally the trio heard the steps come into the room. Whoever it was flipped the light switch and the old-fashioned crystal chandelier lit up the room with a sparkling, almost magical radiance.

Through the opening Carter could see the figure pause at the table. He couldn't make out who it might be but, from the steps and the shape, he was sure it was a man. He tried to get a better view as the figure pulled the front end of the tablecloth up. Slowly the figure opened a small drawer under the table. The boy couldn't see the man's face but he knew the long black hair that covered it. He turned to Penny, who was not in position to see what was going on in the room. Carter mouthed "Mortimer" to her. She nodded. She had expected as much.

Mortimer removed a small, leather-bound volume from the drawer. He held the book up in the light of the lamp and studied the cover for a moment. Then he looked around him as though he knew he was being watched. He stared at the tapestry where the three hid and took a step toward them. Carter and Penny stood quite still, not even breathing. Despite the shadow in which they hid, Penny noticed that Carter's face had turned white with fear.

Mortimer shrugged his shoulders. Tucking the book away in his black leather jacket he turned to the table and noisily shut the drawer. He dropped the cloth over the table once again and moved toward the door. He paused, and then turned the light out. With that he stepped out of the door and strode quickly away down the hall, his steps ringing carelessly in the passageway.

Carter looked over at Penny and the now-visible Merlin. "That was close! Do you think he knew we were here?"

"I don't know," the enchanter responded. "He most likely knew someone was in here, or had been in here, since the lock was gone." He reached over Carter's head and swept the curtain aside. "After you."

The kids stepped out into the room with Merlin following after them. Carter immediately walked over to the table and pulled the cloth back. Opening the drawer he saw that it now held nothing. He closed it and let the cloth fall back into place. "Well, Mortimer got what he came for, I guess." He turned to the enchanter. "Do you know what that book was?"

Merlin nodded. "It looked very much like a magical diary. I think Mortimer is interested in Belinda's work down here." He glanced around the room, "And so am I."

"Then maybe we should get a hold of that book," Penny responded.

The old man looked thoughtful. "Yes, of course." He stroked down his beard and held on to the end of it for a moment. "Yes, perhaps I should pay Uncle Mortimer a visit tonight."

* * * * *

Before Carter had a chance to ask his mom if Penny could spend the night again, Mrs. Blume had already invited her. The girl ran home to pick up a few things and then settled in the room next door to Carter's. "Now we can keep an eye on your great uncle," Penny said. She seemed to be enjoying this adventure while Carter just wished that he'd never met Mortimer. Things were getting too strange, and dangerous, for his taste.

Merlin stayed in Carter's room during dinner. The boy managed to sneak a couple of pieces of fried chicken and a small container of mashed potatoes and gravy for his guest without his mother knowing about it. Merlin smiled when Carter set the food and a bottle of water out on the desk. "I hope you like it," he added.

"Of course I will. Thank you." With that Merlin picked up a chicken thigh, breathed deeply of its delicious combination of spices, and ate hungrily. "Your society has learned how to cook since Arthur's time." He picked some breading crumbs out of his beard and started eating the mashed potatoes. "Mmmm...the cooks never got these so creamy in my time," he exclaimed, with his mouth still half full of potatoes.

Penny grinned. Obviously table manners had also changed since the time of Arthur. But she had no intention of informing the hungry magician of that.

Merlin picked up the two large chocolate chip cookies that Carter had also brought. He sniffed them, and then took a bite out of one. The cookie was soft and full of dark chocolate. A look of ecstasy came over his face. "These are a most magical food. What do you call them?"

"Chocolate chip cookies," Carter answered, smiling. "Good, aren't they?"

"Exquisite," Merlin replied before he stuffed the rest of the cookie into his mouth. He gazed at the other while he chewed and swallowed. "Is it difficult to find these delights here?" He took a huge bite of the next cookie.

Penny laughed. "No. Mrs. Blume baked them at home. She's a wonderful cookie baker."

Merlin savored the last bite of cookie. "What a gift, to make such delicacies."

Carter nodded. "I guess so." He made a mental note to ask his mom to make more cookies for the next time he saw his new friend.

The enchanter drank deeply of the bottled water and wiped his mouth on the last clean paper towel. "Ah! That was a good repast. I thank you again, young master." He rose and stretched. "I must leave you for a little while. I promised to pay a visit to Mortimer and now it is time to fulfill that duty."

"You remember the room he's in?" Carter asked. Earlier that day Mrs. Blume had insisted that her uncle stay at the mansion.

"Yes." Merlin moved to the door. "Don't wait up for me. It may take a while."

The children wished him luck. The enchanter popped out of sight. "Goodnight, my dears." The door opened and closed softly.

Penny pulled a computer game out of her bag and sat down at the computer. "This is a new one. I thought you'd like it." She showed him how to play the game. "It's really a lot of fun."

This was the game Carter had wanted to play for a long time. Penny gave him the computer chair while she pulled up an antique padded stool with a red dragon embroidered on it. Carter made a pretty good start, racking up a surprising number of points for a first time player, but he soon became distracted. He couldn't keep his mind on the game anymore. Instead his attention wandered over the day's events. He still carried his grandparents' picture in his jacket pocket. What had his great aunt done to them? And what was Mortimer doing with that book? He hoped Merlin could discover the answers. Maybe he could find his grandparents.

"You're not concentrating," Penny commented after he had died for the fifth time.

"Yeah, I guess not." The boy stared at the computer screen. Smoke rose from the explosions that had killed off his village again. "Your turn," Carter said as he got up to switch places.

* * * * *

Merlin moved quickly but quietly down the halls. Mortimer had taken a room at the end of a deserted corridor on the second floor. The door opened as Merlin approached. Though invisible, the enchanter stopped and flattened himself against the wall. He did not know if Mortimer had the ability to see him or not.

"Is that you, Clarice?" Mortimer called softly as he stepped out into the hall. He gazed straight through Merlin but seemed not to see him. He did pause for a moment, as though he felt someone was there. Then, turning to the door, Mortimer locked it and walked down the hall into the bathroom. Merlin could hear the toilet flush and the sound of the faucet running as he hurriedly unlocked the bedroom door with a wave of his fingers, slipped into the room and locked the door behind him.

Mortimer returned shortly. He picked up the leather volume he had taken from the Chamber of Art and sat down in a paisley-covered, overstuffed chair. Merlin moved to stand behind him. He gazed over the man's shoulder and read the last entry made by Belinda.

"Finally I am ready to release Merlin from the wood. I have hired men to bring the door to the Chamber tomorrow. Then, tomorrow night, I shall begin this great work. Soon, I shall have what I want, my own sphere of power."

Mortimer stared at the page for a moment then shut the book with a sharp snap.

* * * * *

Carter paced the floor behind the computer chair where the girl sat, writing emails to her friends. "Penny, do you think we ought to try to find Merlin?"

"No. He said he would be awhile." She sent the last email, closed out the program, and shut the computer off.

"Right. He did say that."

The girl stood and stretched. "I'm going to bed." She picked up her backpack. "It's late and I'm tired," she said through a yawn.

Carter glanced at the clock. "Yeah, you're right. It's 1:30 in the morning." He was not a night person at all, but tonight he did not feel tired.

Penny opened the door and turned back to her friend. "Goodnight, Carter."

"'Night, Penny," he answered as the girl shut the door behind her.

Sleep seemed to elude Carter as he tossed and turned in bed. He thought he finally fell asleep and dreamed that someone was chanting far away. The sounds bore no resemblance to English. Suddenly he heard an insistent whisper in his ear.

"Wake up!" came Penny's voice. She shook his shoulder. "C'mon! Do you hear that?"

Carter sat up in bed. The chanting continued. It seemed to come from the heating vent. Penny hurried to the door, gesturing for Carter to follow. The boy stuffed his feet into his slippers and tried to hurry around the bed. "Ow!" he exclaimed as his shin scraped against the bed frame.

"Shhh!" Penny held her finger to her lips.

Carter rubbed his shin a moment then moved to the door. "Ready now?" Penny whispered. He nodded his head. They slipped out the door and headed down the hall to the stairs, trying not to let the boards creak beneath them.

When they arrived at the long hallway on the first floor, Penny snapped on her flashlight. They hurried down the corridor until they came to the turn into the narrower passage. The girl paused, stopping Carter with her hand. "Listen," she commanded in a low whisper. The chanting had ceased.

"It must have been coming from the Chamber of Art," Penny said. Carter nodded in agreement. "Let's hurry. Maybe we can catch whoever it is." The girl pointed the flashlight down the hall and strode quickly behind the beam.

The trek down the passageway seemed interminable despite their speed. The children continued along until the chanting started up again. For a moment they stopped and listened. "It's not Latin," Penny commented.

Carter cocked his head. "It doesn't sound like any language I've heard, and Mom speaks a lot of them."

"C'mon." Penny started off again at an even faster pace. Carter found it difficult to keep up with her at first but he finally settled into the pace just as they were passing the room that contained Merlin's belongings.

The chanting stopped again. Penny slowed to a cautious walk. "It's got to be the magic room," she whispered. They walked in silence until they reached the turn, beyond which lay the Chamber of Art. The two crept up to peer around the corner. The hall was empty. Penny turned off the flashlight, crossed to the other side of the hall and flattened herself against the stone wall. She gestured for Carter to follow.

Silently they moved along the wall where the magic room door stood tightly shut. Penny crouched and listened at the door. A thin line of light shone at the bottom of it. For a long time the two stayed there, straining with their ears for any sound. Suddenly they heard a harsh voice mutter, "When I find you I shall put an end to you and your spells." With that there came the sound of a trunk being opened, then shut. Footsteps moved toward the door.

Penny and Carter scrambled back around the corner. The girl peered back at the door. Carter lay along the floor and cautiously looked around the corner with her. The door opened and out stepped Mortimer. In the light from the room the children could see him clearly as he glanced up and down the hall. He turned back to the room and switched off the light. Now they could barely make him out in the darkness. They heard the key in the lock, and then steps as Mortimer made his way down the hall in the opposite direction.

When his footsteps had faded out of hearing, Penny turned the flashlight on again. She shone it carefully down the passage in the direction in which Mortimer had gone. No one was there. Gesturing for Carter to follow, the girl made her way to the door of the chamber of art. "Locked," she said.

In the pool of light from the flashlight Carter could make out something moving at the bottom of the door. "What's that?" he asked, pointing down. His friend shone the light down at the floor. A huge centipede moved out from under the door, looking like a sea creature as its multiple, feather-like legs, waved around it, propelling it forward into the center of the light.

"That's weird." Penny shook her head. "All the centipedes I've ever seen run from the light, not into it." The centipede looked up at them and waved its legs.

"Now what's it doing?" Carter's face took on a puzzled expression.

"It looks like it's waving at us." The girl stooped down to get a better look. "What? Oh!" Penny stood suddenly and pushed on Carter's chest. "Move!" The boy stumbled backwards into the wall as his friend stepped back out of the way. Something was rising from the centipede. The two stood with mouths open as Merlin appeared before them.

"Thank you for making room for me," the enchanter said, as he straightened his robes.

Carter stared from the magician to the ground and back again. "You—you were that centipede?"

Merlin nodded. "And a handsome one, I might add."

"Uh...yeah." Penny slid her hands into her jean pockets. "I've never seen one so big before." She cocked her head at him. "How did you do that?"

"A little something I picked up in my early training," the enchanter answered with a wink. "Let's head back to your rooms. I'm rather tired. That was a lot of walking for a creature with so many legs."

The three walked back down the passageway, Penny's flashlight leading the way. The girl glanced up at Merlin, who had a thoughtful expression on his face. "What was Mortimer doing in that room? We heard the chanting and followed it down here."

Merlin told them how he had found Mortimer's room and described the passage he had read in the book Mortimer had taken from the Chamber of Art. "He took the book with him and headed for the room," he continued. "I followed but he slipped through the door so quickly that I couldn't get in behind him. I had to change into a more convenient shape to enter the Chamber. I watched as Mortimer placed a scrying mirror on the table and began the spell for visions."

"What's a scrying mirror," Carter asked.

"A black mirror where one can conjure images. It's useful for seeing just about anything you want to see, if you have the gift and the proper training." Merlin stroked his beard with his fingers. "Obviously, Mortimer has both."

"So," Penny began. "What did he see?"

"Avalon, the place where Arthur lies." The enchanter started slowly down the hallway again.

The children followed. "Avalon?" they both asked in unison.

77

"Avalon. You have many stories about it. Avalon is an ancient city. Arthur was taken there after he received his mortal wound."

"What did Mortimer see there?" the girl asked, a little impatient for an answer.

Merlin turned back to them. "The nine ladies who guard Avalon." He stroked his beard thoughtfully again as they continued down the hall

"Nine ladies?" Carter repeated. "Who are they?"

"The guardians of Arthur as he sleeps and...keepers of the ancient knowledge, a knowledge that would be dangerous in the wrong hands."

"Is that what Mortimer is after?" Carter asked.

"That I cannot say. His desires are hidden for the time being, but I have no doubt that he will act on what he has seen tonight." With that the enchanter quickened his pace. Penny and Carter hurried to keep up with him.

CHAPTER ELEVEN
Merlin at School

Carter awoke to the sound of his mother's voice at the door. "Time to get going!" she called cheerfully. "We have to leave this morning."

"Okay, Mom. I'm getting up," the boy called sleepily. He looked at the clock, rubbed his eyes and looked again. Nine a.m., he thought. Not much sleep for going to bed at four o'clock that same morning. "Merlin," he called softly. "Are you here?"

No answer came from the air around him. "Guess he doesn't need as much sleep as normal people do," Carter murmured to himself as he flung the covers back and slid his feet to the floor.

Carter arrived last for breakfast wearing his customary blue jeans and sweatshirt. His sneakers squeaked on the floor as he strode into the kitchen. Penny waved and said, "Good morning" through a mouthful of toast.

Mrs. Blume smiled. "Sleep well?" she asked him as she spooned fluffy scrambled eggs onto his plate.

Carter sniffed the eggs hungrily. "Uh, yeah, sure, Mom." He began to eat with great appetite, grunting his thanks when his mother set a couple of pieces of buttered wheat toast on his plate. Suddenly he felt a hard kick on his leg under the table. "Oof!" He glared over at Penny.

"What was that for?" Mrs. Blume asked.

Carter glanced at his mom. "Oh, I...uh...just bit my tongue, that's all."

"You seem to be doing that a lot this weekend," his mother commented, shaking her head.

The boy gave Penny another dirty look, which she returned with an even harder kick. As soon as Mrs. Blume had

79

turned back to the stove Penny gestured to Carter's right with her head. The boy looked in that direction just in time to see a piece of toast rise from the plate of extra toast his mother had just set on the table. He glanced from the floating toast to his mother, who still had her back turned, and back again. The toast floated down the hall and out of sight.

The boy breathed a sigh of relief and continued to eat his breakfast. He put some of the scrambled eggs in a plastic bag on his lap. Merlin needed more than a piece of toast for breakfast.

When the three had finished eating Carter slipped the bag of eggs and a bag of buttered toast under his bulky gray sweatshirt. He opened a drawer and grabbed a fork when his mother was busy at the sink. "Gotta go pack," he said as he hurried out of the kitchen.

"We're leaving in an hour," Mrs. Blume called after him.

Merlin gratefully ate the breakfast Carter brought up to the bedroom while the boy stuffed his things into a small suitcase and his backpack. "Merlin?" Carter asked in a tentative voice.

"Yes?"

"Were you planning to stay here after we leave or...or would you like to come home with me?" The boy paused. "Uh...we will come back here next weekend, of course. Mom's got a lot more to do."

The enchanter smiled, his eyes sparkling under his bushy white eyebrows. "I was wondering if you would ask." He nodded. "Yes, I'd like to see your home."

* * * * *

Outside Penny, who had come over to say goodbye, tried not to show her feelings, though she was loathe to see them go. "See you next week, Carter."

"Yeah. 'Bye, Penny," Carter responded. He would miss his friend. He started toward the car with his suitcase and backpack.

Penny couldn't see Merlin but she felt his presence in front of her as she stood in the yard outside the kitchen door. Mrs. Blume stood several yards away, packing the car and talking to Carter. The girl took the opportunity to say goodbye to Merlin. "I'm glad you're free now, Merlin," she said in a low voice. "Will you be back next week?"

"At least by then, my dear girl. And..." Penny felt the enchanter's whiskers brush her forehead as he kissed her gently on the top of her head. "Thank you for your help. Farewell for now."

"Farewell," Penny whispered.

* * * * *

On the drive home Carter sat in the front next to his mom to keep her from looking in the back seat where Merlin might be doing who-knows-what while invisible. Thirty minutes into the drive Carter glanced back to see Merlin trying to work an electronic black jack game. The boy caught his breath when the game began to make noise. Obviously Merlin had figured out how to win.

Lucky for them both his mom liked to keep her eyes on the road. "I didn't even know you were playing that, Carter," his mother said. "Did you win?"

"Umm...yeah. I won. But I'm tired of playing it now," the boy answered, shooting a meaningful glance back at the enchanter. Out of the corner of his eye he caught sight of the game returning to the pouch on the back of his seat. Carter relaxed a bit, until he felt Merlin rummaging around in the same pouch looking for something else to do.

"Actually, Mom, I really love looking out the window at the scenery," he said with an emphasis he hoped Merlin would catch. The rummaging stopped.

For the next hour Merlin remained mostly still, cautiously stretching his legs out now and then as quietly as possible. Carter hoped the enchanter would find the ride fascinating and figured he would spend a lot of the time looking out the windows at the new world he had so recently entered.

Mrs. Blume pulled into the drive-through at a fast food restaurant. "What do you want?" she asked Carter.

"I think I'd like a grilled chicken sandwich, a spicy chicken, two cheeseburgers and two fries." His mother stared at him in surprise. "Uh, I'm pretty hungry, ya' know. Guess I'm a growing boy." Mrs. Blume smiled at that. "Oh, and could I have two sodas?"

"Certainly, my growing boy." His mom smiled and turned to place her order.

Mrs. Blume nibbled on chicken nuggets as she drove while Carter ate his food out of the bag. When he was sure his mother wasn't looking he would sneak food back to Merlin in the space between the back of his seat and the car door. Merlin quietly took the two sandwiches, drink and extra fries. Carter hoped his mom couldn't hear the sound of the ice as it knocked against the sides of Merlin's cup. He wondered why he seemed so sensitive to sounds, even the slightest ones, all of a sudden. The crackle of sandwich foil sounded so loud that he knew his mother had to hear that. He began talking about anything he could think of to distract Mrs. Blume.

"Hey, look at those cows. What are the brown and white ones called?" the boy asked.

"Guernsey, I think. Looks like they've got a few llamas, too." His mother smiled at her son's new interest in farm animals. She had grown up playing on her best friend's family farm and treasured the sights and smells of her childhood.

Carter glanced back at Merlin. He saw the soda cup floating behind his seat. "Uh, what do they do with llamas, anyway?"

"Well, usually people raise them for the wool." Mrs. Blume raised her soda cup and took a long sip. "I would rather raise sheep or cashmere goats." She took another sip.

"Cashmere goats," Carter murmured, still feigning an interest in farm animals. "They sound soft."

"They are, and the wool sells for a good price." Mrs. Blume raised the straw to her lips and had just begun to drink when a loud slurp sounded in the back of the car.

Carter froze for a moment, then grabbed his cup and slurped the last bit of drink from it. Actually, it was more melted ice than soda.

"That was loud," Mrs. Blume complained. "I thought I taught you better than that."

Carter shrugged and put his cup in the holder. "Guess I was just too thirsty to be polite. Sorry."

Mrs. Blume shook her head.

Two hours after they had left Aunt Belinda's house they finally arrived home. As the car nosed into the driveway a seven-year-old girl ran out of the house to greet them. She stood smiling and laughing as her mother turned off the engine and climbed out of the car. "Mommy!" the child shouted and threw herself into Mrs. Blume's arms.

"Peggotty, my little cupcake!" Mrs. Blume answered with delight, swinging her daughter in a big circle. She was still a strong, athletic woman.

Carter took advantage of the diversion unwittingly provided by his kid sister to open the back passenger door and let Merlin get out of the car. He heard cracking sounds as Merlin stretched and muttered, "Such a cramped way to travel, but much better than horseback for a long trip."

"Watch out," Carter whispered. "Here comes my sister." Peggy ran over to Carter and gave him an enthusiastic hug, which he returned. Peggy could be annoying, as little sisters often were, but she was also gifted with a sunny disposition and a charm that few could resist.

"Carter! I missed playing ball with you, and computer games!" She stood back, smiling at her brother. The smile faded slightly as she looked to Carter's right. She glanced curiously back and forth from Carter to the space to his right. The boy froze, thinking that she might be able to sense the presence of the magician, who stood exactly where his little sister was looking. Then the girl's face brightened and she took Carter's hand. "C'mon! Dad bought us a new game while you were gone!"

Just at that moment, Mr. Blume walked out the front door and embraced his wife, and then stooped to hug Carter. The boy's dad, Carter Senior, was a lanky six feet and two inches, pretty tall compared to his shorter offspring. He had the same mop of curly dark hair that his son had. His eyes were gray, with a distinct dark line around the iris. Carter's brown eyes also had that ring. "Well, my boy, it seems that you had some adventures at Great Aunt Belinda's. Find any ghosts lurking around?"

Carter smiled hesitantly. Well, no ghosts, he thought, except for that weird dark smoke. But as for enchanters...he just hoped Merlin would stay out of the way of his active family.

Merlin wandered off as soon as they walked into the house. He had whispered to Carter that he wanted to explore the house on his own, and very pointedly murmured that he would stay out of the way. The boy wondered if the enchanter could read all of his thoughts. "No," the old man replied. "Just the loud ones, remember?" Carter did remember the last time Merlin read his thoughts. They must have been loud, too.

The alarm went off too early for Carter the next morning. "Man! Already?" the boy mumbled as he swung his legs over the side of the bed and padded off to the bathroom. At breakfast he managed to pack Merlin's breakfast in his lunch bag so he could give it to him when they got out of the house. Carter's school was just a few blocks away so the two set out walking. The boy pointed out a small park where Merlin could eat in privacy. "We left early so we have enough time for you to eat breakfast," Carter said, handing a bag of pancakes to the enchanter.

"Mmmm....this looks good." Merlin appeared just as he sat down on a park bench. Carter took a double take. Merlin no longer wore his robe. Now he sported a multi-colored tie-dyed tee shirt and bellbottom jeans, topped off with a Green Peace baseball hat.

"Where," the boy began, "did you get that outfit?"

Merlin grinned. "I can transform my robe into any suitable clothing." He glanced with pride at his apparel. "Yes, I studied clothing styles for the past fifty years in your father's library last night. I liked this style best, and the freethinking philosophy that went along with it. The hat makes a statement, since, despite all of the knowledge humans have gained, people continue to destroy the natural world around them."

Carter nodded. "It looks just right on you. In fact, there are a lot of old hippie guys around here. You'll fit right in!" The boy explained how classes worked at school and that Merlin would have to stay invisible on school grounds. "Otherwise they might call the police on you. They're pretty paranoid these days."

During Carter's first class, American History, Merlin sat in the empty chair behind the boy. Occasionally he would whisper a comment about the revolutionary war, which was the day's topic. At one point he muttered, "Even with guns these people clung to old ways of doing battle. I remember teaching Arthur to change fighting styles according to the terrain and types of enemies. Not that he always listened to me..."

"Mr. Blume," the teacher interjected, cocking his balding head to one side. "If you have some enlightening information about this topic then please share it with the class."

84

Carter felt like a trapped animal, pinned to his seat with his teacher's harsh gaze. "Uh, I was just...um...just talking to myself, Mr. Baldwin." He heard laughter from some of the kids.

"Well, then, why don't you tell us what you told yourself." Mr. Baldwin turned to the laughing class and silenced them with a stern look. Gazing once again at Carter he demanded, "Well?"

Merlin whispered something to the boy.

"Uh, I was just saying that it was pretty amazing that both sides used such outdated battle tactics. I mean, with guns and forest around, the revolutionary soldiers could have used guerilla tactics...which...uh...would have been a good strategy for fighting a larger foe."

Mr. Baldwin's face took on a quizzical look, then a slow smile spread across his features. "Yes, Mr. Blume. Not only were you listening," at this he frowned at the rest of the class for their inattentiveness during his lecture, "you were also thinking. This is something the whole class should be doing."

Carter began to relax in his desk.

The teacher smiled at Carter again. "Next time, young man, I suggest you raise your hand when you have such insights." With that he resumed his lecture.

Second period was English class. The teacher took them to the library to pick out biographies for a report. Carter and his friend, Imani, picked out their books quickly and settled at a back table. "I love Edgar Allan Poe," Imani whispered. She was a bright girl with a reputation as the best catcher around.

Carter shivered. "His stuff is so creepy. Don't you get scared when you read that?"

"No." Imani grinned, her white teeth flashing against her brown face. Her long braids swished as she shook her head. "You are such a scaredy cat!" She pantomimed cutting out Carter's heart and burying it under the table. She moved her hand up and down on the table whispering, "Thump-thump, thump-thump, thump-thump," to remind him of "The Tell-tale Heart."

The boy scowled and flicked her arm with his finger. The two quickly opened their books as the teacher walked by the table. When she was gone Carter glanced around, looking for Merlin. Out of the corner of his eye, he saw a book rise off a shelf and disappear into a far corner of the library.

Once class was over Carter said good-bye to Imani and hurried to the boys' bathroom. "If no one is in the boys' room we can talk there," he whispered to the enchanter. "What do you think of school so far?" A couple of older girls in the hallway gave him an odd stare. He paid no attention as he hurried into the bathroom.

Fear gripped him. Three of the school bullies stood near the sinks. One of them put out a cigarette in a stream of water. Pekoe saw him first. "Well, look what just crawled in here." He spat an obscenity at Carter, who began backing toward the door.

Roger, the biggest of the three, laughed. "I think he's scared of us." He gestured toward the toilets. "How 'bout a swirly, little girl?" Carter backed another step, memories of being held over the toilet by these same boys flashing through his head.

Pekoe, who went by his last name because his first name was Gabriel, started toward him. The third boy, Tom, edged toward the door to block Carter's escape. Carter glanced around him in hopes of glimpsing Merlin but he could see nothing of the invisible enchanter. The boy whispered, "I think we can take them all with your help." A half-smile crossed his lips for an instant.

"Now he's talking to himself." Pekoe laughed a cruel laugh. "Do you have an invisible friend? Don't worry, we'll flush him down the toilet, too!" With that the bully charged. Before he could grab him, Carter kicked the boy in the belly with all his might. The force of the kick threw Pekoe back into a urinal. The boy hung with his face and arms in the urinal, stunned, with the breath knocked out of him.

Roger stared, a look of anger mixed with shock purpling his square face. He was a foot taller than Pekoe, of a thick, stocky build. Most kids in the school feared him and stayed out of his way. Carter glanced from Roger to Tom, who stood in a martial arts fighting stance. He was more excited than scared, seeing how Merlin had helped him kick Pekoe across the room.

Roger threw himself at Carter, grasping for the boy's throat. The impact jammed Carter back against the wall. The back of his head made a dull thud against the cinder blocks. For a moment he was stunned. Then he felt the air choked out of his windpipe by the bully's big hands. Carter panicked. He had to get air.

Merlin, this would be a good time to help me, he thought. Suddenly he felt a surge of strength. He swung his arms up and outward, then down across the bully's arms, breaking the boy's grip on his throat. Carter grabbed Rogers's shoulders and pushed him away from him. The huge bully flew back against the opposite wall and crumpled to the floor. To Carter, the older boy suddenly looked very small.

He had no time to think about that. Tom yelled a "hayah!" and leaped toward him, his leg cocked for a powerful jump sidekick. A strong hand reached out and grabbed Tom's leg in mid-leap then tossed him on the floor. Tom landed in a heap under the first sink, stunned and breathless.

"Well, Carter," said the tall, blond-haired boy who bested Tom. "I could see you didn't need any help but I thought I'd get a piece of the action, too." He grinned, his blue eyes sparkling, and slapped Carter on the shoulder.

"Thanks, Jack. I didn't mind the help at all." Carter glanced from his friend to the bullies groaning on the bathroom floor. Pekoe pulled himself up, spitting out pieces of urinal cake. He moved painfully to the sink and began rinsing his mouth.

"Look, boys," Jack began. "You better leave this guy alone. He's the best outfielder and batter I've ever met. If you bother him again you'll have to answer to the entire baseball team...that is if Carter doesn't beat the tar out of you first." He put his arm around Carter's shoulder. "Let's get out of here and let these jerks recover."

With a last look at the bullies, Carter nodded and left the bathroom. He hoped Merlin could read his thoughts as he thanked the enchanter fervently in his mind.

CHAPTER TWELVE
The Crystal Portal

Carter walked thoughtfully down the front steps of the school, streams of his fellow students pouring out the door around him. He made his way to the playground and looked around. It was deserted. Suddenly he caught sight of a flash of color as Merlin waved at him from behind a nearby tree just off the school grounds. Carter hurried to join him.

"Ah, my boy, such an odd way to try to educate children," the enchanter commented. He still wore the hippie-style clothes from earlier in the day. "I did get a lot of reading and web surfing done at the library." He shook his head. "So much knowledge is available to anyone who wants it now. This age has much potential."

Carter looked up into the enchanter's sparkling eyes. "Thanks for helping with those bullies in the bathroom today."

Merlin gave him a quizzical look. "Whatever are you talking about? I was in the library most of the day."

Carter was stunned. "Three bigger boys attacked me in the bathroom. You must have been there because I was able to fight them off." He fixed his gaze on the enchanter. "It had to be you, otherwise, how could I have thrown them across the room?"

"How could you not with such power as you have?" The enchanter smiled approvingly. "And it appears to be growing every day since I met you."

The boy shook his head vigorously. "No!" He said adamantly. "I could never have done that. Then I would have fought them off before."

"But you were younger then. Perhaps you are beginning to understand that you have more power available to you than you once thought." Merlin put a hand on his shoulder and steered him

88

toward the sidewalk for the walk home. "Come along, young mage. Your mother is expecting you."

Young mage, Carter liked the sound of that. He straightened up and walked proudly beside his wise, elderly friend. They continued in silence when a familiar car pulled up to the curb next to them. Mrs. Blume waved. "Hi, honey! Did you have a nice day?"

"Uh, yeah, Mom. It was fine."

Carter's mom looked Merlin up and down suspiciously then glanced back at her son. "Is this someone you know?"

"Oh, yes," the boy responded. "I met him a while ago." Carter's mind raced, hoping he could keep his mother from finding out who his companion really was.

"So then, what's your friend's name?" she asked.

Carter thought frantically, kicking himself that he hadn't thought to have a name ready for Merlin for just this purpose.

Merlin stepped closer to the car and held out his hand. "The name is Myrddin ab Morfryn."

"Oh? That's an interesting name. Where is it from?"

"Wales, my dear."

Mrs. Blume relaxed a little and shook the enchanter's hand. "Well, very nice to meet you Mr. uh..."

"Morfryn." Merlin bowed elegantly, too elegantly for a hippie guy, Carter thought.

Mrs. Blume nodded politely. She turned her head toward her son. "I'm on my way home, Carter. Want a ride?"

Carter shook his head. "I'd rather walk, Mom. Thanks anyway."

* * * * *

When the two arrived at the house, Merlin became invisible again. "I hope it doesn't hurt you to be invisible for so long," the boy said quietly as they walked to the front door.

"No, but I have to pay close attention to what I do, as you well know." Carter waited for Merlin to pass through the doorway before slipping into the house himself. He could hear the rustle of the magician's robe as he turned around to whisper, "By the way, I could really use something to eat, my boy."

89

"Sure. I was thinking the same thing, too."

* * * * *

The week passed quickly. Friday afternoon arrived, finding Carter and Mrs. Blume packing the car for another trip to Aunt Belinda's odd house. Merlin seemed more than ready to return. He told his young friend that he had work to do in the Chamber of Art. "What is it?" Carter asked, stuffing the last pair of socks into his backpack.

The enchanter eyed the boy for a moment and smiled. "You'll find out soon enough as I think I will need your assistance on this. And the young lady's as well."

Carter's eyes gleamed with excitement. "You mean that me and Penny can actually help you?"

"I thought that was what I said." Merlin gave him a quizzical look. "I sometimes wonder if I have quite learned this modern English of yours." He was about to continue but the sound of Mrs. Blume's voice from downstairs cut him short.

"C'mon, Carter! We have to get going. I want to get there before dark."

The boy grabbed his backpack and hurried out the door. "Coming, Mom!" he called. Looking back at Merlin he saw him disappear and felt him pass near him through the doorway.

By late afternoon they reached the old house. Apparently Mortimer, who had been staying there over the past week, had cleaned up the old branches and other debris in the front yard. Newly planted chrysanthemums sprung from the front garden in mounds of gold, purple and white. Pansies of a multitude of colors lined the edge of the flowerbed. Carter smelled the strong and pungent scent of new pine mulch.

"How lovely!" his mother exclaimed as she gazed at her uncle's work. "Isn't he something?"

Oh, yeah, Carter thought. He sure is...but not in the way his mother thought. Well, it was nice to see the softer side of the strange man. Of course, it really meant nothing, considering that he was working against Merlin and the magical Avalon.

"Ah, Clarice! So good to see you," Mortimer called in his cool voice as he stepped out the front door to greet them. Glancing at

Carter he added, "And you, too, grand nephew." The boy muttered a hello.

Clarice hurried up the steps and gave her uncle a hug. "Mortimer, those flowers are beautiful!"

Mort smiled his thin smile. "Thank you." He stepped back to get a better look at his niece. "And you, Clarice, you become more lovely by the day."

At this Mrs. Blume blushed. "Thanks."

"Come in, both of you." He patted Carter on the shoulder. "I have baked some cookies—with the same family recipe your mother uses. I just hope I got it right," and he glanced at Clarice, who smiled again. Carter tried to look interested but he wasn't even sure if he could trust any food Mortimer cooked. He found the image of his strange uncle baking cookies incongruent with his suspicious image of the man.

Once in the house, the boy's mouth watered involuntarily as he smelled the delicious scent of fresh-baked cookies. Well, his uncle probably wouldn't poison them...at least right off. He ate three of the cookies with delight, the dark chocolate melting on his tongue in just the right way. He felt fine after eating them. He saved a few more in his pocket for Merlin.

"Mom, can I go see Penny now?" Carter made his way to the back door, anticipating his mother's answer.

"Oh, of course," she replied. "Uncle Mort and I have a lot of estate business to get to anyway." With that, Carter was out the door and halfway across the yard before Merlin made his presence known.

"I noticed you put some of those wonderful cookies in your pocket," the enchanter began.

"Sure did." Carter handed the cookies into the air. One by one the cookies floated up and disappeared in large bites. The boy giggled to himself. "Merlin, if you could see what that looks like..." But before he could continue his thought Penny called out and ran to them.

"Carter! Merlin!" she cried, putting an arm around the enchanter even though he was still invisible. She had seen the last cookie rise and disappear, knowing it had to be Merlin causing that particular phenomenon.

Carter couldn't hold back his excitement. "Penny, Merlin needs our help in some magic stuff."

"Cool!" the girl responded. "When?"

The enchanter's voice drifted quietly out into the clean fall air. "Tomorrow night, my dears. I will need your help tomorrow night."

They continued on their way and quickly arrived at Penny's house. Old-growth oaks, maples and hickories stood proudly round the home displaying their brilliant fall foliage in various shades of gold, orange and red. "Lovely trees," Merlin commented. "Your family must take good care of them."

Penny smiled, glancing around at them. "We love them. I've helped feed and trim them since I was a little girl." The trio made their way noiselessly up the stairs to Penny's room. Once the door was shut Merlin appeared in green robes instead of his usual purple ones. The two kids stared at him expectantly.

"I must return to Avalon so they may know I have been released from my prison of so many years." He nodded graciously to Carter. "And, if it is your wish to accompany me, I would very much like to introduce the young man who gave me my freedom, and the young lady who helped him," he nodded toward Penny, "to the women who guard Avalon and its treasury of knowledge."

Penny gasped. "We're going to Avalon?" Carter sat speechless, his mouth partly open as if he meant to say something but just forgot.

"More than that," the enchanter continued, smiling, "I wish to familiarize you both with your heritage, human and faerie. Whether or not you choose to train in magic, you have earned the right to know more about the old ones who came before us."

* * * * *

Clarice sat in the kitchen, gazing out the window. "More tea?" Mortimer asked.

"No, thanks. I better get back to work." She brought her attention back to the files she had laid beside her cup on the table.

Mortimer placed a kind hand on hers. "Clarice, it can wait another hour. You are still tired from your trip."

92

Suddenly the front doorbell rang. "I'll get it," Mortimer said, and hurried down the hall to the foyer. Clarice recognized the oily honey tones of Miss Nimway. She was as persistent as she was annoying. No, she had gone far beyond annoying at this point. As Mrs. Blume rose and made her way to the door she wondered just who this woman thought she was, coming here so often when she had been told not to do so.

Uncle Mort would not let them in. Instead, he stood firmly blocking the doorway while Stonehurst apologized profusely for their unwelcome presence. Miss Nimway interrupted her partner. "We are anxious to give you top dollar on many of Belinda's antiques. She had the finest taste and we don't want to see you swindled by these American dealers, always trying to get something for nothing. You know how people can be so greedy."

Mort did not step aside as his niece came up beside him. "Ah, Mrs. Blume! So nice to see you," Miss Nimway exclaimed, her gaze moving from the woman's face to the small spherical pendant that she always wore around her neck. Her eyes still on the necklace, she smiled almost to herself. "Yes, such a lovely lady you are, too."

Mortimer's eyes followed Nimway's gaze. The pendant glittered in the late afternoon sunlight, which seemed to light up the sphere from the inside. Mort turned a steely glare to Nimway. "There is nothing for you here," he said evenly in ice-edged tones. "We have not even finished our inventory."

"Yes, I'm sure there is much to be done," Stonehurst interposed with a conciliatory air. He gently pulled at Miss Nimway's arm.

"Well, we will be here a little longer but we must return soon to England." Miss Nimway followed Stonehurst's lead, turning to walk down steps. At the bottom of the stairs she turned back to say, "Remember, top dollar." Then they left.

*   *   *   *   *

Carter had been given permission to stay over at Penny's that night. Merlin left at around ten that evening, saying he had things to prepare for tomorrow's adventure. The kids talked late into the night about what they might see in Avalon and how excited they

93

were about going. Finally they wished each other goodnight and went off to their separate rooms.

Penny's sleep was disturbed by strange dreams. At first she found herself running frantically through a dark forest. Many heavy feet ran after her. She stumbled in the darkness over fallen tree branches, vines, and underbrush. Her heart pounded in her chest. She called out for help.

Suddenly a woman appeared before her in an aura of sickly reddish light. Her long black hair covered her face. Her robes were of crimson, with black and gold trim. She beckoned to Penny. "Come, I will protect you." Penny took a step forward. The woman reached out with her hand but it was rotted like that of a corpse. The girl screamed.

The next thing she knew, Penny was kneeling in a courtyard, bound hand and foot. The woman stood over her and laughed cruelly at the girl's plight. She held up a beautiful sword. "Before you die you should know who took your pitiful life!" The woman threw back her long black locks, revealing her pallid face.

"It's you!" Penny cried. "I know you!"

"Of course you do." She raised the sword over her head. "And now I shall end your meddling ways." The sword swung down toward Penny's head. Penny screamed.

* * * * *

"Penny! Wake up! You're dreaming." Carter shook her by the shoulders. "C'mon, Penny. Wake up!"

The girl's eyes opened. Her vision was so blurry at first that she could barely make out Carter's face, much less Merlin's, as they hovered over her. She sat up quickly, almost colliding with Carter's head. "I know who she is!"

"Who's what?" Carter asked.

"She had this beautiful sword and…and…" Penny paused. Her eyes opened wide. "That's it! She's the one who tried to kill that man in his sleep! It was his sword!"

Merlin leaned toward the girl. "Maybe you had better start from the beginning."

Penny took a deep breath. "One night the electricity went out. I was looking in that mirror over there." She pointed to it as it

94

gleamed softly in the semi-darkness of the room. "I saw three women in robes and long hair looking into a bright sphere. I looked, too, and saw a man lying on a bed holding a sword."

Merlin drew a quick breath and murmured, "Then it is about Arthur."

"Arthur?" the kids asked, puzzled.

"First, I must hear the rest of your tale, young lady." Merlin listened carefully as Penny recounted the vision in the mirror and then the frightening events of her dream. At the end of her story she leaned back against the pillows as though speaking had drained her of energy.

"Well," she began, her eyes on the enchanter. "What does it mean?"

"You said earlier that you knew who the woman was." He stroked his beard absently. "Do you recognize her?"

Penny nodded excitedly. "Oh, yes! She's Miss Nimway. I saw her in the mirror and in my dream." Merlin pursed his lips and stared at the wall. "She was just awful, Merlin!"

He stood and faced the two. "You have no idea to what lengths she will go to accomplish her will." The enchanter began to pace slowly back and forth across the room.

Carter had listened to Penny's story with a mixture of terror and amazement. He rose from where he had been sitting on the bed. He struggled to keep his voice calm. "What should we do?"

Merlin stopped pacing. "I must find a way to stop her."

"I'll help you," Penny and Carter said, almost in unison.

The enchanter shook his head. "I fear that I may bring you into terrible danger."

"Please let us help," Penny urged. Carter nodded his agreement.

Merlin gazed at them, a smile curling at the corners of his mouth. "You both are brave and noble people. With your gifts you could be a great asset to me."

"We'll be careful," Carter added.

"Yes, you will have to be," the enchanter agreed. "Indeed you will. So, get dressed. We have to leave immediately."

Penny jumped out of bed and reached for her closet door. Carter hurried out of the room, his eyes sparkling with the thought of the adventure ahead. He tried not to think of the danger as he dressed and ran back to Penny's room.

* * * * *

Mortimer woke suddenly. He knew something was happening, though he could not hear anything besides the normal settling noises of the house. He slipped out of bed and changed his clothes in the dim light of a single candle. Reaching into the drawer of his nightstand, he pulled out the antique box, set it on the dresser and opened the lid. He murmured words in an ancient tongue and drew out a strange, rectangular pendant on a leather string.

Raising it over his head he whispered, "May the one who wears this gain power and protection." Mortimer let the pendant fall around his neck, blew out the candle and hurried out of the room.

* * * * *

Merlin strode down the long but now familiar corridor. Penny and Carter walked quickly on either side of the enchanter. The three hardly exchanged words until they reached the Chamber of Art. Merlin grabbed a cord that hung next to the tapestry behind which they had hidden a week ago. "Carter, my boy, pull on that rope over there." He gestured to the other side of the tapestry. While Carter pulled on the rope, the enchanter pulled strongly on his. The tapestry rolled up along the wall as if it were a window shade.

Merlin switched off the electric light and took the now glowing sphere from his robe. Walking to the false doorway, he beckoned to the children. "Come. Stand in here."

The light from the sphere revealed a beautiful sight. Penny gasped as she looked around the arch of the portal. It glowed as the light reflected in hundreds of deep purple amethyst crystals. "Whoa!" Carter exclaimed in an excited whisper, as he stepped into the doorway. Purple light colored all of them, as if they, too, were part of the crystal clusters.

"Ah, yes," Merlin commented. "I had almost forgotten how beautiful these portals are."

"Portals?" Penny asked.

The enchanter nodded.

"Are there more of these?"

"Oh, yes." Merlin held the sphere up to give them all a better view.

Carter shook his head in amazement. "I've never seen anything like it!"

"No," Merlin answered. "But perhaps you will see more of these in the future."

Penny started to ask a question but the enchanter raised a gnarled hand. "We must go now. We can discuss portals at another time, my dears." With that he reached up to the top of the arch almost touching it with the sphere. "Now it is my turn to show you wonders."

Purple and white light began to swirl around the portal, lazily at first, and then faster and brighter. Wind rushed by them, in wild gusts that raced faster and faster, yet at the center Carter felt that he was moving and thinking in slow motion. Dazed, the boy looked around him, noticing a wisp of black smoke in the light. The wind turned him round and round until he could hardly bear the dizziness. Then all sensation ceased as he lost consciousness.

CHAPTER THIRTEEN
The Island of Apples

Suddenly, Carter found himself swaying inside a different portal. Penny and Merlin had already stepped out and now watched him, a strange woman at their side.

"So, you are with us again," the enchanter was saying with a grin. "Quite a ride, don't you think?" He reached for Carter's hand. "Come, now. The dizziness will wear off soon."

The woman smiled at the boy. It was a kind smile that made him want to smile back, but all he could manage was a groggy, crooked grin.

Merlin guided him to the woman, saying, "This is Amera. She is one of the nine ladies who protect and maintain Avalon."

"So, we're there? I mean here?"

"Yes," Amera answered. She was a lovely, ageless woman in a flowing, sea green gown. At her throat she wore a ruby in the shape of an apple. The leaves of the apple sparkled in pure wrought gold and the apple hung from a silver bough. Smiling, the woman took his hand in both of hers. He felt a warm feeling flood his body. Suddenly his head cleared.

"Wow! I feel so much better!" He glanced from Amera to Merlin, who smiled and nodded toward the woman. "Thank you," he murmured, still hardly comprehending what had just happened to him. He gazed around. The walls of the room glowed a soft blue. They seemed almost transparent.

Amera spoke to Carter. "If you are ready, there are some people who have been very eager to see you."

"Me?" the boy asked, amazed that anyone in this magical place even knew about him.

"Oh, yes. Follow me." With a kindly smile at Carter, the woman turned and walked toward the middle of the wall. The trio walked after her. As Amera approached the wall a doorway suddenly appeared. Penny and Carter looked carefully at the edges of the doorway as they walked through it.

"The wall just disappeared," Penny exclaimed. She gazed in wonder at the doorway as it suddenly became part of the wall again. "How does it do that?"

"Avalon is a place of magic," Amera began. "The Ancient Ones left much of their advanced knowledge and technology here."

They walked down a wide, comfortable corridor. The walls here were sky blue and shaped like a large tunnel. "It's almost like walking in the sky," Carter whispered to Penny. She nodded.

As they turned a corner they entered an emerald green corridor, similar to the first except that the top of the walls bore a metallic trim of red apples, green buds, and pink flowers on silver boughs with copper-colored leaves. Penny let her fingers brush the walls as she walked. "It's so smooth, almost silky," she commented aloud.

"Yes, these walls are made of a special material that the Ancient Ones often used in their cities." Amera stopped walking and touched the wall herself. Smiling, she turned to the children. "We do not know what they are made of so we cannot reproduce them. We believe that your scientists may be only a few hundred years away from recreating similar technologies."

Only a few hundred years? That sounded like a long time to Carter. He had so many questions, but no idea of which one he should ask first. He cleared his throat, a little nervously. "Uh, what's with all the apples on the wall? And on your necklace?"

The woman put a hand to her throat and gently grasped the ruby apple, holding it up for them to see. "Apples represent Avalon. Years ago this place was called 'Insula Pomorum', Latin for 'The Island of Apples.'"

"I read about that," Penny began. "Apples were a symbol of immortality, weren't they?"

"Yes," Merlin answered, pleased that Penny had studied some of the old traditions of Avalon. "They were also thought to bring love to those who knew how to use its powers."

99

"Love magic?" Penny grinned as she glanced over at Carter. The boy appeared startled at her look. Then he blushed a deep crimson.

"Yes, among other uses, they were often employed in spells that would bring suitors to a young lady's door." Merlin chuckled quietly as he watched Carter stare off in another direction, pretending to be interested in a brass sculpture of an apple tree further down the hall.

In an instant the moment was forgotten when the group heard voices calling to them. Carter recognized the two figures who hurried towards him. "Grandma!" he cried. "Grandpa!"

"Carter, my boy!" Michael Griffin grabbed his grandson around the waist and picked him up as easily as if the boy were no more than a toddler. Carter laughed and hugged his grandpa around the neck, ruffling the old man's thick gray hair. He had always wondered at his grandfather's strength. Though he stood tall, at about 6' 2", the old man appeared slender—no—wiry, as Grandpa used to put it. Mr. Griffin put the boy down and patted his head. "How you've grown!"

"Indeed!" cried a melodious voice next to them.

Carter turned and gave his grandmother a hug. "I missed you both so much!" he said through the tears that began to trickle reluctantly down his cheeks. "We all thought you were dead. Mom still cries sometimes when we talk about you."

Marguerite, who was only a little shorter than her husband, pulled out an embroidered handkerchief and gently wiped the tears from his face. Dabbing her own eyes, she smiled brightly. "We couldn't understand why we seemed stuck here every time we tried to return. We missed our family terribly. I tried not to think of how it must have felt for all of you, especially Clarice."

Carter stepped back and gestured to the rest of the group. "This is my friend, Penny." Marguerite held out her hand. The girl grasped it warmly. Carter turned his eyes to the enchanter. "And this—"

"I could never fail to recognize the one we have striven so hard to protect," Michael interrupted. He bowed in deep respect. "Lord Merlin, it is an honor to finally meet you." He took the enchanter's gnarled yet powerful hand into his own.

Merlin nodded, smiling broadly. "I am indebted to you and your fine wife," he said, turning his gaze on Marguerite, "and to your family's loyal efforts through the long years of my imprisonment."

"Well," Carter began. "Not everyone was loyal..." He trailed off and gave Merlin a meaningful glance.

Marguerite looked up into Merlin's sparkling eyes. "We never knew what happened, or why we couldn't return. Can you tell us?"

The enchanter took a long, slow breath and told the story of his release from the door and explained the binding spell Belinda had used to keep her sister and brother-in-law in Avalon. He described the visits by Nimue and Stonehurst and how they had posed as antique dealers in an attempt to get the door, and to also gain entrance to the old house. Merlin asked Penny to tell the Griffins about her vision in the mirror and the dream she had about Nimue.

Grandpa Griffin spoke first. "So, you think Mortimer may have been part of Belinda's scheme?"

Penny nodded. "He did seem pretty suspicious. His shoes looked like they fit the footprints outside that night when someone broke into the basement, and he had the same kind of mud on his shoes."

Michael rubbed his smooth chin for a moment. "But Nimue's plot has nothing to do with Belinda, or Mort for that matter, if I remember him correctly." He exchanged a meaningful look with Merlin.

The magician pursed his lips, and then answered the look. "No, hers is a more sinister plan."

At that Amera stepped around the group and moved a few feet into a new corridor. "Come." Without a word the group followed. They turned down another passage whose walls were of pure white, opalescent with occasional streaks of gold, silver and blue. Amera stopped at a green portal. She held her sphere in front of the door and said her name out loud. The portal disappeared and the group walked into a dark green chamber. Here the walls looked as though they were made of malachite, with swirls of varying shades of green, accented by curling streaks of rust red. Penny and Carter gazed in wonder about them.

Meanwhile, Amera walked over to a green console and placed her sphere in a malachite holder. She spoke in a soft but firm voice into the console, speaking a language that neither Penny nor Carter had heard before. "There he is," Amera announced in a reverent voice. The group turned to the back wall, which suddenly became transparent. A bed, covered with a rounded, silver-tinted casing, stood in the middle of the next room, whose walls were of an opaque blue, sparkling here and there with golden flecks. Within the casing a man lay in peaceful slumber.

"Who is that?" Carter asked. Suddenly he noticed the sword the man held with both hands resting on his breast.

"Arthur," Merlin murmured. He turned to his young friend. The tears in his eyes made them brighter than usual. "It is my boy... and my king." The enchanter wiped his eyes on his sleeve.

Penny gently laid her hands on his arm. "I'm so sorry," she said in a quiet voice.

Merlin turned to gaze again at the sleeping man lying in state on the covered bed. "I haven't seen him since we went our separate ways. I had warned him about Mordred. He refused to listen to anything I had to say. He kept insisting that Mordred was the only son he had and that the boy would learn to be a king if he came to live with him." He shook his head.

Penny moved to Amera's side. "That was in my dream, but he seems to be safe."

"He is for now."

"Why do you keep him here?" Penny asked.

Amera gazed at Arthur. "We keep him because he made that choice. Long ago, when Arthur lay dying at the Battle of Salisbury Plain, The Lady of the Lake herself went to see him. She offered him a choice. He could die as every man did, or he could stay at Avalon in an unconscious state until the time when his own rare gifts were needed again. In this state, between waking and sleeping, Arthur would also be given the chance to leave his body and travel in spirit form to advise the rulers of Britain."

Penny gasped. "That's why the legends all say that Arthur would return in England's time of need!" She shook her head and added, "but he never came during the two World Wars...or any other time when Britain needed him."

"He did, indeed." Amera held the sphere over a smaller sphere built into the console. "Arthur visited many of Great Britain's leaders in dreams, during both wars. Some paid no attention, thinking such dreams were nothing more than flights of fancy. Churchill, however, was one of the men who took much of his advice to heart. He wrote about it later in a personal letter to a friend." She looked at Carter. "That friend was your grandfather's own father."

Penny moved toward the transparent wall to get a better look at the legendary hero. "I had no idea," she murmured in a low voice.

Amera spoke in the strange tongue to the wall before her. Immediately an emerald green portal appeared. The woman strode to the portal and held the sphere up in front of it. The door disappeared, leaving an open doorway into the chamber where Arthur slept. She turned to the group and beckoned them to follow her.

Arthur lay in serene repose upon silken sheets of gleaming silver. Penny looked closely but could see no signs of the man breathing. His hair and beard were well trimmed, his clothing fresh. His hands crossed over his breast and over the pommel of the great sword that lay lightly upon him. At his head a very large sphere pulsed with white light.

Merlin stood, gazing at Arthur for a few moments. Then he patted the case, turned, and left the room. After a few minutes, Amera silently led the rest of the group out of the chamber.

* * * * *

Mrs. Blume enjoyed a quiet breakfast that morning. She felt certain that her son and his friend were having a good time at the Morgan house. As she sat in the breakfast nook sipping her tea, she thought about the strange powers that had passed from generation to generation in her family. Clarice smiled when she remembered how surprised her husband had seemed when she first used her power in front of him to create a beach scene in their bedroom on a cold winter day.

She fingered the small crystal ball at her throat. Though Clarice had chosen not to receive anything more than the most basic training in magic from her parents, she felt quite content with what she knew. For her, a loving husband and two healthy children were the greatest magic of all. She wanted very much to have the time to focus on them.

In seven more years Carter would come of age. She wondered if he would want to have the training that she had refused. Clarice smiled. She had known her son had some of the family power since the day he first played catch with her. Noticing that Carter caught the ball every time she threw it, she had tested him by throwing it a little further away from her son. Each time the ball would change direction and land inevitably in the boy's hand. Despite his demonstration of telekinesis, Clarice held to the family tradition of waiting until his eighteenth birthday to inform him of the faerie bloodline that he shared.

The sound of the doorbell roused her from her reflections. She got up and hurried to the door. As she opened it, she quickly wished she had not. There stood those two irritating antique dealers, again. "How many times do I have to tell you I'm not interested in doing business with you?" she exclaimed in frustration.

Miss Nimway fixed her cold, gray eyes on Clarice. "You will let us in, now, my dear."

Clarice, her eyes suddenly vacant, seemed held by the older woman's gaze. "Of course," she replied, and opened the door obediently.

As Nimue stepped into the house her tailored suit fell away into mist, leaving the woman in a translucent gown of black trimmed in silver and red. Stonehurst remained as he was, but now he wore a silver chain with a large silver medallion that bore an inscription in the ancient Ogham alphabet.

Nimue continued to hold Carter's mother with her gaze. For each step forward, Clarice took a step back, caught like a hapless insect in a spider's web. Finally, Nimue backed her victim to the velvet-covered divan in the parlor. "Sit down," she commanded. Clarice obeyed. "Now," the sorceress ordered with a sweet smile, "give me the pendant you wear."

The younger woman put her hand over the sphere for a moment then silently unclasped the chain. Taking the necklace in her hand she paused, as though trying to fight off the spell that held her fast in its inexorable grip. Then she put out her hand and dropped the sphere and chain into Nimue's waiting, grasping hand.

"Now, my dear, it is time for you to sleep." Nimue's voice returned to the honeyed tones of her earlier visits with Clarice. "Sleep until dawn, my sweet, then, if no one comes to awaken you by then, your sleep shall transform into that greater and more blessed sleep...the sleep of death." The sorceress touched the young woman on the forehead.

Stonehurst hurried to catch her as she fell sideways off the divan. He laid her down gently on the rug. "Such a shame they will not return in time," he murmured.

CHAPTER FOURTEEN
The Stolen Sword

Amera guided her guests to a soft orange-hued dining area. The walls here seemed made of pure carnelian. Round tables with matching chairs appeared to sprout from the floor of polished river stones. In the center of each table stood a rounded box, open in the front. "Ah, I remember the food here," Merlin began. "I think you shall all enjoy it."

Carter sniffed the air, puzzled by the odd lack of food smells. Maybe whoever ran the kitchen hadn't started cooking yet. Though his stomach growled, he tried not to think of his hunger. After all, it might take a long time to prepare whatever it was they were going to eat. Unless the people of Avalon didn't eat real food. He tried not to think of that, either.

"Please sit down," Amera said, gesturing to a large table in front of them. Everyone took a seat. Penny plunked herself down on her chair and grinned happily at Carter, who seemed rather suspicious of the chairs that appeared to be made of clear glass. He sat down carefully, wondering if the chairs could break easily.

Amera seemed to read his thoughts. "No, my young friend, these furnishings are constructed of a material similar to the plastics of your world, only they are much stronger and have special properties that we can adjust at will. We may not know how to make them but we have learned how to work with what the Old Ones constructed long ago."

"Do you use the spheres for that?" Penny asked.

"Yes."

Carter broke into the discussion. "But why don't you share this cool stuff with our world?"

The woman smiled patiently. "We strive to preserve these technologies from generation to generation, but we have yet to understand them. The Ancient Ones warned against allowing them to be shared until most humans developed minds that could focus clearly and without self-serving intent."

"That will take a long time," Penny commented wryly.

Merlin gestured to Marguerite, who nodded and placed her hand on the box. She closed her eyes for a moment, then opened them and withdrew her hand. Suddenly, a tray of food appeared in the box. The older woman took the tray out, sniffed its contents appreciatively and set it down in front of her.

"Ah," her husband sighed. "You've chosen the beef burgundy. Excellent! I think I shall get the same." He placed his hand on the box and then took up the tray that appeared.

Amera chose only a fruit salad. Merlin grinned at the two children, who by now were wide-eyed with curiosity about the source of the food. "All you have to do is concentrate on the sight, smell and taste of the food you want. The processor uses the ingredients that are in its storage compartments to produce what you want to eat."

"Well, I'm a vegetarian, so I guess I'll order up some tofu or something." Penny paused. "Can it do that?"

Amera smiled. "Give it a try, my dear."

Penny placed her hand on the smooth, green surface. It felt cool, like a gemstone. Closing her eyes, she focused her mind on a delicious Hunan bean curd she had eaten a couple of weeks ago. She opened her eyes when she realized that she was no longer imagining the smell. It was real. "Cool! I'd love one of these at home!"

"Well," Carter began. "I hope that they still have some beef left in that machine, 'cause I just want a hamburger." The boy placed his hand on the box and a juicy hamburger, complete with bun and a side of fries, materialized. "Wow! This smells great!" Carter grabbed the hamburger and took a bite, chewing with ecstasy.

"Actually," Amera pointed out. "None of the meat dishes are really made from animal flesh." Carter stopped in mid-chew and stared at the woman. Smiling, Amera explained. "We grow everything in our greenhouse complex. The meats are really composed of soy, grains and other vegetables." She noticed that

107

Carter had not resumed eating. "Go ahead, young man. It tastes just like you imagined it would." With that, he finished off his lunch, enjoying every bite.

Almost everyone had finished eating when Amera suddenly stood up, her hand at the apple pendant at her throat. "I'm sorry. We must go immediately!" She turned and hurried from the room. The group rose and followed quickly. No one spoke. Merlin strode beside Amera.

"Something terrible has happened," the woman said in a quiet voice. "Someone has broken into Arthur's chamber." At that, Merlin took her by the arm and quickened his pace.

An elderly woman with long, silver hair greeted them at the door of the green room where they had seen the sleeping king just minutes ago. "Granuaile." Amera grasped the other woman's hand. Granuaile returned a strong clasp.

"Branwen was struck unconscious and her sphere was stolen. See her there." She pointed to a lovely young woman lying still on the floor in front of the console. Her gauzy green robes lay like clouds around her slender body. Merlin took a step toward the injured woman when Granuaile put up a hand to stop him. "Merlin," she began in a firm voice. "It is much worse than that." The old woman swept her hand in a gesture emphasized by the purple and gold sleeves that floated about her arm. "Excalibur is gone, too. And the Lia Fail."

Merlin's eyes widened at the news. He stepped to the open portal and walked to Arthur's side. Yes, the sword had been taken from his sleeping grasp. The monarch's arms lay where they had fallen. At Arthur's head the large, glowing sphere was gone; its bowl-shaped holder lay empty. The enchanter turned to Granuaile. "Who has done this?" His voice trembled with anger.

"We must ask Branwen," she answered, indicating the young woman who had begun to awaken under Amera's ministrations.

Merlin returned to the control room and knelt upon one knee next to Branwen. She sat on the floor, her head resting against the side of the green console, her face pale. "I...I didn't see them until they were upon me," she murmured. "They tried to kill Arthur but his enclosure shut too quickly."

"How many," Merlin asked.

"Two, a man and an older woman."

Penny gasped. "How did they get here?"

Granuaile looked hard at the girl. "Who?"

"Nimue and Stonehurst, of course." Penny shook her head. "Did they use the portal, too?"

Merlin rose. "If they used the portal..." He trailed off, staring at Carter. Placing a hand on the boy's shoulder he continued, "They had to have access to a sphere. A small one would have worked."

"Small sphere?" Carter shrugged. "Where?" Merlin looked straight into his eyes. The boy's eyes widened. "My mother wore a sphere...a pendant." He finished the thought. "They took it from her, didn't they?" His eyes took on a pleading look, as if the enchanter could undo whatever Nimue had done to his mother.

Merlin nodded and spoke softly. "Yes, that is probably what they did. As for your mother, we must hope for the best."

"But she is in danger!"

"Perhaps, but we must first find Nimue and Lord Stonehurst," Merlin said. "The objects they have stolen contain great power."

"Yes, that is so, but there is more." Granuaile moved to the doorway and turned to the group. "Without the great sphere, what is called the Lia Fail from ancient Celtic legend, our city will not have enough power to withstand attack."

"Those two have the power to take over Avalon?" Penny asked.

"Yes," came the answer. The old woman's voice took on an air of finality, "We must prepare our defenses."

*   *   *   *   *

The wild grasses stirred in the noonday breeze. The air carried the crispness of autumn, but not the biting chill. Clouds gathered overhead, as they did almost every day in England. A stone manor house looked out upon the tranquil scene. Its front door opened and two figures came striding through the long grass.

"Now is the time for our triumph!" Lord Stonehurst exclaimed, his bloodshot eyes gleaming. He shifted the weight of the yew-wood pedestal in his arms. The green marble top came loose. The man shifted again, just in time to save the top from falling to the ground.

Nimue gave him a scornful glance. "The work has only begun, Henry, you simpleton." She turned to face him. Gesturing with her long, slender fingers toward her partner's heavy load, she spoke a single command, "Levitate!" The pedestal pulled itself from Stonehurst's grasp and floated in the air between them. Henry's face took on a sheepishness that looked quite out of character for his strongly English features. The woman turned and continued to walk, the black leather bag at her side swinging with her steps.

"I was about to do that," the man sputtered in embarrassment. "I just wanted to see if I could carry it in...uh...the traditional manner."

"Yes," Nimue answered scornfully. "You love to show off your manly muscle power. I often wonder if you have learned any magic at all."

"I have studied..." Henry began then let it go. He knew only too well the dangers of arguing with her. The woman walked on as though he were nothing more than a bothersome fly.

They continued through the grass to an ancient yew that stood on a small rise in the center of the field. Under its curving boughs the two stopped, the pedestal still hanging between them. The sorceress pointed to a shallow depression in the ground. "There."

Stonehurst used his hands to guide the pedestal over the spot, and carefully, now using his levitation skills, set its end in the depression that had been dug for it. "Alright, then. Now we have that in the ground." He wiped his face with a white handkerchief, glancing at the thickening clouds.

Nimue nodded. She stooped to bring the Lia Fail from its hiding place in the bag she carried. Holding it up in the darkening light, she stared into its depths. "It roared for kings once. Now it shall serve me, and scream for all the world to hear when I take up my own throne." The sphere, about ten inches in diameter, was much larger than the spheres carried by Merlin or the ladies of Avalon. It glowed white, with a spectrum of colors swirling in its center.

She raised the globe with ease, as if it weighed very little, and murmured in a strange language. She set it into its resting place in the green marble top, carved like a shallow bowl to accommodate the object. The swirl of colors grew until the whole sphere glowed. The light grew until it lit up the entire area under the old tree, and the shimmering colors played on the faces of the two partners. Smiling, Nimue turned to Henry. "Now to complete the portal," she said as she pulled Branwen's sphere from her coat pocket. She handed it to Henry. "You know where it goes." He nodded.

Henry walked out onto the field where a stone arch stood. He had constructed it himself before they had left England, using some magic, of course. As he neared the structure, he gazed with satisfaction upon his handiwork. Clusters of amethyst crystals gleamed around the inside of the arch, as well as in the threshold on the ground. Three stone steps led up one side of the structure. Stonehurst stepped up onto them and carefully placed the sphere into a cavity at the top of the arch. There it began to glow in purple and silver light, growing brighter and setting the crystals on fire.

For a moment Henry seemed awed by the brilliance and beauty of the light. Then, Nimue's voice broke in upon his reverie. "Come back here, you old fool! We have work to do!" Automatically, he turned back to the hill where the yew tree's branches seemed to burn with the colors of the sphere it sheltered.

Nimue took her place behind the pedestal, her face, hair and eyes glittering with the colored light. The sphere she wore at her throat amplified the effect. She had taken up the sword, Excalibur, and now raised it over the large sphere before her. The sword glowed red, as if it had just been pulled from the forge in which it was cast. Stonehurst hurried to stand to the left and a little behind the sorceress. She murmured rhythmically in the ancient Brythonic tongue, repeating the spell over and over until her voice rose to a shrill scream that echoed sharply around them.

At that, the ground began to tremble. Strange wisps of smoke seeped from the earth. Each one grew and thickened to the point that they seemed about the size and shape of a man. The sorceress stood in a blaze of color and light, exulting in the power of the moment, feeling the shuddering ground beneath her feet. She cried out, "Ha! My victory is near!" then lowered the tip of the sword so that it pointed straight out from her body and over the field. She began to chant again in the strange language. She repeated the verses of her spell three times before she uttered the words in English. Each time she repeated the spell her voice grew stronger and louder until the entire field reverberated with her words.

Warriors, from this grave arise!
See, I give thee soulless eyes.
I give thee bones that will not break,
And putrid flesh, for hatred's sake.
Take up sword, halberd and spear,
March through this portal, Avalon's near.
Lay her secrets open to me,
I'll take the powers of her sisters, three.
Destiny's stone, my desire fulfill,
So every creature shall serve my will.

Nimue's eyes rolled to the back of her head. Lightning shot from the Lia Fail into her chest, traveled along her arms and through Excalibur. Thousands of streaks crackled out over the field, each striking one of the shadowy figures standing there. The lightning roared as the field seemed to explode in light.

Then the light dimmed and its sound died. Now a loud humming noise grew from the large sphere before Nimue. The woman relaxed and lowered the sword. She smiled as she surveyed her handiwork. Upon the scorched grass stood soldiers from a long-forgotten battle. Their flesh was decayed and covered with infected wounds in which maggots crawled. They stood in tattered kilts or leggings, bearing the weapons they had wielded on this field long ago, among them swords, pikes, battle-axes and shields. Their dead eyes fixed on Nimue as they raised their voices in a shout of allegiance, "Victory to Nimue, our Queen!"

At that the sorceress raised the sword and pointed it to the portal, whose light began to swirl in a mesmerizing spiral. The Lia Fail hummed louder and louder. A powerful beam of purple light shot with red struck Nimue in the chest again, down through Excalibur and right into the portal. The hum grew in intensity, the pitch climbing higher and higher until it could barely be perceived by the human ear.

"Go, now, my warriors!" Nimue cried, her body trembling with power. "Go!" At that the army began to move, forming ranks.

Stonehurst stood transfixed by the terrible sight and the power wielded by his partner. Nimue laughed, her head back, her shining black hair streaming behind her. "Does this frighten you, Henry?" He struggled to turn his gaze away from her, but found himself firmly caught in her power, as if he, too, were one of the lifeless soldiers.

As the warriors marched to line up three abreast before the portal, the ground trembled with the dull thudding of their feet. Their eyes now fixed on the portal with its swirling light, they marched into it and disappeared. As more and more of them departed from sight, the thudding sounds subsided, until, at last, they were all gone.

CHAPTER FIFTEEN
Battle for Avalon

Penny stood with her back against the green wall, gazing at the prone figure of Arthur. Suddenly, out of the corner of her eye, she saw something move. She turned to look at the wall to her right where swirls of purple and red light had appeared. Thinking she was just seeing things, the girl blinked her eyes and looked away for a moment. Looking back at the wall she saw soldiers marching through the light and into a hall that looked like one of the ones she and her friends had traveled to get to this room.

"What do you see, child?" Merlin asked quietly. He had watched the girl as Penny's eyes had become transfixed by the vision.

"They're coming here!" Penny cried. She pointed at the wall, "And they're horrible!" She tried to pull her eyes away from the grotesque figures but could not.

"What—" Merlin stared at the wall, unfocusing his eyes so that he could see into Penny's vision. "They are the dead of an ancient battle once entombed in a mass grave."

Granuaile stepped to the girl's side, reading the vision from Penny's mind. "Each side had fought hard against the other. Then their bodies were placed side by side in dead comradeship."

"Nimue has done this," the enchanter declared. His face paled. "Excalibur…"

Penny looked at him, fear in her eyes. "Are they coming here?"

The old woman touched the apple pendant at her throat and closed her eyes momentarily. Opening her eyes, she gestured for the group to follow her. "I have alerted the guardians. We are all in danger." Her pace quickened. "Hurry. They have just entered our city."

The group ran down the varicolored halls, a muffled sound of heavy feet growing louder by the moment. As they turned a corner, Granuaile stopped them suddenly with a gesture. Carter ran into her strong arm, which now held him back. He glanced at the woman, and then turned his eyes to the sight in front of him. Warriors with ancient weapons marched toward them, their dead eyes fixed straight ahead. One of their numbers saw the group and pointed toward them, crying out in a forgotten tongue. Now the rest turned their gaze fully on the ladies and their guests. Carter stared in horror as the stench of rotted flesh hit him in the face. Penny grabbed his arm and pulled him back around the corner.

The ladies turned and ran with surprising speed back down the hall from which they had just emerged. The rest of the group hurried after them. Granuaile did not speak, but Penny thought she caught a few of the telepathic commands. "Amera, to Arthur's chamber," the girl heard in her head. "Branwen, with me to the control wing."

Granuaile lead them quickly through a series of corridors until the sound of tramping dead feet faded down another hall. They had lost them. "Merlin," Granuaile whispered. "We'll need your help to secure the city's defenses." The enchanter nodded. "Michael and Marguerite, go with Amera to guard Arthur. Nimue shall surely want him dead so she can break his connection with the Lia Fail."

"We understand," Michael whispered, and Marguerite nodded her assent.

Amera turned to the group. "May we see each other again, in victory." She raised a hand in farewell then turned to run down the hall, her robes streaming after her like banners of blue-green and gold. The Griffins followed, keeping a surprisingly quick pace.

Granuaile led the rest of the companions down several more corridors, each larger and more impressive than the last, until they finally came to a huge chamber that housed strange constructions of spheres, crystals, and multiple shapes of the same material which made up the city walls. "This is the master control chamber. We can defend the city from here." She took a sphere from her robes and set it down in a circle with seven other spheres on one of the consoles. The ninth spot, where Branwen's sphere should have rested, lay empty.

Merlin stepped up to the console and laid his sphere down to complete the circle. A humming sound began to fill the chamber. The enchanter turned to Penny and Carter. He answered the question in their eyes. "These spheres will boost the power grid so that the protective fields around the city may better withstand assault."

"Yeah, but those awful warriors are inside," Carter observed. "What are they going to do about that?"

"I suppose," Penny began, "that they have force fields inside, too." She glanced at the enchanter with a hopeful expression. "Right?"

"Yes, but the warriors have broken through two already." He frowned. "Without the Lia Fail the rest of the barriers will not last, especially against Excalibur and the great sphere itself."

As Carter gazed around him he watched several women in shimmering robes working at consoles throughout the chamber. Branwen operated the one to his left. She inserted a series of crystal shapes into the top of her control panel. The entire console lit up with the colors of the rainbow. The light traveled up into the center structure, a large, onion-shaped ball with many tubes attached to both the top and the bottom. As the women worked, the room became filled with light and color. Carter had to shield his eyes when he gazed in the direction of the central structure.

The humming grew louder, but that was soon drowned out by a new sound, that of the warriors battering at the door. The women all looked up from their consoles for a moment before returning to work. Granuaile, standing at the main console where the spheres lay, motioned to Merlin. He stepped quickly to her side. "You know that this room must be protected at all costs." She had to shout above the din. "If Nimue takes the controls here she will be able to defeat our sister cities."

"Yes, I understand." Merlin turned to his young friends, a shade of sorrow in his eyes. They looked up at him, frightened, yet at the same time, willing to help. "Come with me. We have a difficult task ahead of us." He strode to the far wall and waved it aside. There stood a small room lined with shelves of strange, crystalline objects.

Penny stepped closer to investigate. "They look like swords and spears out of crystal." She gazed around her in wonder.

Merlin grabbed a large crystal sword. "Take what you think you can use," he cried, girding on another sword in a royal blue scabbard.

Carter put on a sword in a red scabbard and snatched up another sword. "How do we use these things? Don't they have better weapons than this?"

"No," the enchanter responded. "All of the other weapons were destroyed after the great war that melted the glaciers thousands of years ago."

Penny gripped one sword and wore another in a purple scabbard. "Maybe that wasn't such a great idea, because we could sure use some laser guns or something."

Merlin hurried from the armory with the two close behind him. The pounding grew louder. He paused at the door and turned to his friends. "The barrier is almost down. Once we get out there we have to be ready to fight." They nodded, uncertainty showing in their young faces. "I didn't think it would come to this when I brought you here," he said regretfully, "but our destiny lies before us. We must do the best we can."

Carter glanced from his sword to the enchanter. "I don't know how to use this."

Merlin smiled sadly, his eyes bright with suppressed tears. "The weapons will intensify your powers as well as your concentration. You, my boy, must use your telekinetic abilities to wield those swords." Turning to Penny, he took a deep breath. "And you, my dear, will be able to see the opponents' moves before they strike. You can defend against them and strike before they do." Penny nodded, gripping her sword more tightly.

Without another word, Merlin turned to the door and waved it open with his hand. Suddenly the three stood before the terrifying foe. The door closed behind them just as the barrier in front of them gave way. They raised their swords as the first few leapt to engage them. The enchanter fought with amazing fury, parrying the strokes of all of the first warriors at once. He snatched the other sword from his side and brought it into play as well. He moved with a grace that belied his years, striking, parrying, striking and slashing, felling the warriors before him.

By now the entire barrier had disappeared. Penny flung up her sword as two of the decaying men attacked. She could see, in her mind's eye, the strokes they intended to inflict upon her. She swung her sword to strike and thrust at them before they could do the same. One fell at her feet while the other continued to beat at the girl's defenses. Suddenly she stabbed him full in the chest. A yellow liquid shot from the wound, splattering on her and spraying Carter, who had just raised his sword to fend off his first enemy.

"Yuck!" Penny cried. She sidestepped the falling soldier and took on another two. "They're disgusting!"

Carter's nose wrinkled at the putrid stench from the liquid. The warriors smelled rotten already, but now the repulsive odor intensified as the trio slashed open the animated corpses. The boy had no time to complain, however. He threw up his sword to parry a blow then recognized an opening to strike. The sword obeyed his thought immediately, thrusting deep into the warrior's abdomen. Fear clutched at Carter for an instant, long enough for the staggering soldier to slash at his head. The boy regained his concentration and knocked the sword from his opponent's hand so that it only grazed his cheek.

The sudden pain in his face put the boy's mind in better focus. He knew that failure to focus on his task would kill him in an instant. He pushed fear away and fought with a new intensity, his sword moving as swiftly as his thoughts.

Carter's arm grew heavy. Sweat poured down his face and his clothes felt sopping wet as he continued to defend against the untiring foe. He hardly noticed the humming from the control room and the barriers that still stood around the city. The crashing of sword against sword seemed no more than background noise. The dead army made no sound as they fought, not even cries of pain from the blows of the three living fighters.

As if in a dream, the boy wielded the sword in his own internal silence. He slipped the second sword from its sheath and brought it into play just as one of the warriors knocked the other sword from his right hand.

"Carter!" He heard Penny cry out as if from a distance. "Carter!" This time Penny's voice sounded clear and quite close. The boy slashed and stabbed at the soldier in front of him. As the warrior fell, Carter stooped to snatch up the fallen sword. He glanced at Penny.

118

"C'mon!" she cried over the din, gesturing to the opposite side of the hall. She began to fight her way in that direction. Carter followed her lead. Glancing in the direction the girl had pointed, he saw Merlin halfway across the hall, mowing down the enemy like a farmer gone mad in his own fields.

Suddenly, the enemy stopped in mid-stroke. Every one of the decayed warriors turned toward the end of the hall and paused, as if stunned by the light that shot out at them, lighting up the grotesque bodies and faces of the once-slain men. As one entity, they began to march down the hall, swords down, dead faces without expression.

The light slowly began to swirl around the hall, changing from white to violet. The warriors continued their steady march into its whirling depths, leaving the fallen behind them. Carter stood mesmerized by the light, which now reached all the way down the hall to him. He could feel its pull as it circled faster and faster, now more like a tornado that threatened to suck everything into itself. The boy swayed, his arms rising with the powerful current of light.

"Get out of it!" Carter heard the enchanter's voice over the hum of Avalon's defenses, and the stamping of the soldiers feet as they continued toward the center of the vortex. "Get out!" He looked around him to find Merlin. The old man stood at the corner of the hall to the boy's right, gesturing for Carter to come to him.

The front of the army became distorted by the vortex. Their elongated bodies began to swirl like the light itself before disappearing into the maelstrom. Whether or not the soldiers knew what was happening to their fellows, they each moved inexorably forward then grew distorted as the center sucked them into its brilliant depths.

Carter tried to move toward Merlin and safety, but his legs seemed stuck in place. He glanced down. His own body had begun to distort in the swirling light. Fear gave wings to his feet as he strove to run to Merlin's side. Suddenly he turned around, looking wildly up and down the hall for Penny. There she stood, transfixed by the light, her body beginning to elongate as the current reached hungrily to take her, too.

"No!" With no thought for himself, the boy struggled to her side. "Penny!" he cried, grasping at her arm. His hand distorted as he touched her. She did not even look at him.

119

"Penny, you've got to come with me now!" With that he put both arms around her waist and tried to pick her up. The light began to pull them both forward. Carter closed his eyes and focused on bringing Penny away from danger. His eyes flew open when he realized that he had not only picked up the girl, who weighed at least as much as he did, but he had also run almost half the distance to Merlin. His feet felt as though they ran in the air, just a few inches above the floor. He kept his eyes on the enchanter, who now smiled and extended his arms towards them.

"Excellent work, my boy," the old man called as Carter set Penny down on her feet beside him.

"Penny? Are you okay?" The boy's eyes searched her face for recognition.

"Okay? What just happened?" Penny looked around at Merlin and Carter, and then down at her own body. "I felt so...so weird out there."

"You almost followed Nimue's warriors," Merlin responded, pointing out toward the strange scene. The light had diminished somewhat so that the three could make out the outline of a portal much like the one in which the trio had arrived. The sound of marching feet had diminished to the point that they could no longer hear it above the humming that sounded through the hall.

Then the remaining rank of warriors swept into the center of the vortex, just elongated blobs that grew smaller and smaller until the last one disappeared. The swirling light drew itself inside it, then, with a loud "pop", it, too, was gone. Standing behind the portal, Michael and Marguerite together held a sphere that glowed softly in violet and white. They smiled when they saw Merlin, Penny, and their grandson striding toward them. Turning to each other, they kissed over the glowing sphere. Then Michael dropped it into his wife's hands.

Marguerite gently slipped the object into a silken bag at her waist then put out her arms to hug Carter. "You were wonderful out there!" she exclaimed then turned to the others. "You were all wonderful!" She hugged Penny firmly and kissed her on the cheek.

Carter looked over at the enchanter, who grinned back at him. Then Merlin's face quickly took on a serious expression as he addressed the group. "Well done, to all of us. But even though the Griffins have sent these warriors back to the place from whence they came, Nimue can send them anywhere she wishes."

"You have all done us great service," came Amera's voice as she hurried toward them in a swirl of gauzy robes. The five turned to her as she caught her breath and continued speaking over the hum. "Merlin is right; we must find a way to stop Nimue from sending her warriors back to Avalon."

"We must also get the sword and the Lia Fail back from her," Merlin said, his face grim.

"How can we do that," Amera asked, "when even the Lady of the Lake is powerless against it?"

The enchanter gazed at his companions, measuring them with his eyes. He locked on to Michael's steady gaze. "That will be our concern, Amera." Turning to her he placed a gentle hand on her shoulder. "Go, now. Do what you must do."

The woman reached up and touched his hand as if drawing strength from it. "I will go to my sisters." Amera smiled encouragingly at Penny and Carter, then nodded to the group. "Farewell to all of you. Our hopes, the hopes of Avalon and her sister cities, go with you." Without another glance, she turned and hurried down the hall toward the control chamber.

Michael stooped behind the portal whose crystals still glimmered in violet and white. He straightened up, holding a long white bag in his hands. He opened it and offered it to his wife. Marguerite drew out two crystal swords and slid them into the belt at her waist. Michael pulled two more from the bag and stuffed one in his belt, hefting the other in his hand. "It's been awhile," he said, an eager tone in his voice.

Merlin gestured to Marguerite. "Let's go." His voice could barely be heard. Carter put his hands to his ears to block out the hum that now grew painful to hear.

Taking out the sphere, Marguerite stepped into the portal and held it up. Violet light swirled and pulsed around the sphere and in the crystals that lined the portal. The group squeezed into the space as the light grew more intense. Carter felt dizzy as the light transported them out of the hall. A small wisp of black smoke entered the portal and followed them.

121

CHAPTER SIXTEEN
The Talisman

Penny stepped out of the portal. The setting sun cast an unearthly orange glow on the scene before her. She gasped. "Merlin?" she whispered. The enchanter appeared at her side, sword already raised for battle.

"I'm here." He put a reassuring hand on the girl's shoulder. "So, we have followed our foe."

Penny swallowed hard and brought her own sword up to defend against the countless dead warriors that surrounded them. Carter stumbled out just as Penny turned to warn him. "We're right in the middle of them all."

Carter's grandfather grasped his arm. Marguerite took a position at the edge of the portal. Her long gray hair streamed behind her in the wind that had just picked up.

"Back into the portal!" Merlin cried but suddenly their way was blocked by the terrible soldiers. Two of them grabbed Marguerite and put their swords to her throat. She struggled for a moment then stopped as the point of one of the swords dug into her flesh. Blood trickled from the wound as Marguerite surrendered and allowed one of the men to take her sword.

The enchanter glanced from the trapped woman to the decaying warriors all around them. He fixed his gaze toward the tree at the top of the hill before them. Then he nodded his head. "Put your weapons down, my friends." He dropped his sword into the shriveled grass at the feet of the two warriors who held Marguerite. Slowly he drew the other sword at his belt and gently tossed it to the ground as well. Michael and Carter followed suit.

Merlin turned to Penny, who still stood holding her sword at the ready. "Put it down." Penny's red hair flamed in the dying rays of the sun. Her face had taken on a wild look. Merlin moved toward her and quietly removed the sword from her grasp.

"No," she murmured. "We can't give up now..."

Merlin gave her a half smile. "We're not giving up. We're just putting down our weapons." He took a step in the direction of the two captors. Then he laid the sword in the grass with the others. The sun slipped below the horizon.

"Release her!" called a commanding voice from the hilltop.

The soldiers let go of Marguerite, who brushed herself off in disgust. She stared at the woman on the hill. "Nimue! You have no right to use these men!" She gestured around the field. "You desecrate the dead! The penalty for that will be swift—"

Nimue interrupted her. "You would do better to pray for mercy from me. My powers increase the longer the stone is with me." The baleful orange light surrounding the woman grew in pulses until it lit up every decaying face on the field. Now Nimue spoke to the soldiers. "Why have I raised you, mighty warriors? Why have I given you new life?"

A huge shout answered her. "For the glory of our Queen!" The grotesque men began to beat on their shields with their weapons, crying "Nimue, our Queen! For the glory of our Queen!" over and over again until the sorceress raised her hands for silence. The soldiers immediately snapped to attention, their weapons at their sides.

"Yes, my warriors. Your faithfulness will be rewarded." She turned a cold smile on Merlin and his friends. "Come. See what the real use of power can do."

The enchanter gestured for the group to follow him as he began to walk toward the hill. The rest trudged after him in stunned silence. Carter glanced around him to make sure none of the soldiers threatened them. Every warrior stood stock still, staring at Nimue, whose features took on a mask-like appearance in the pulsating light.

Penny pulled a handkerchief from her jean pocket. "Mrs. Griffin," she began, tugging at Marguerite's sleeve. The woman glanced down at her. The girl offered the handkerchief, saying, "Take this. You're bleeding."

The older woman smiled and took the white cloth. "Thanks." She mopped up the blood that had run down the side of her neck and under the collar of her flannel shirt.

"Have you been in battle before?" Penny asked.

"Yes—many kinds of battles." The look on her face hardened as they climbed the hill to stand in the light under the tree.

The girl noticed that Nimue looked much older than she had when they met at the house back home. Home, Penny thought. How far away that reality seemed from the bizarre dream in which she now found herself.

"Ah, Merlin, you bring such powerful warriors with you," Nimue taunted in mocking tones. The sword, Excalibur, rested against the side of the pedestal, reflecting the light of the great sphere along its shining blade.

"Powerful?" The enchanter looked over his friends. Michael and Marguerite stood with the two young people between them, alert and ready to do battle again if necessary. Penny watched Nimue warily, more like a predator than prey. Carter appeared frightened, yet a determined gleam in his eyes told Merlin that he would do everything he could to overthrow the sorceress. "These," he continued with a gesture toward his companions. "These have powers that you can never know in your twisted state of mind."

Nimue's features darkened with a scowl momentarily, before her face once again took on its smiling mask. "Well, we can certainly do without these doddering fools." She touched the sphere, which began to give off small streams of sickly green light. Penny began to feel nauseous as the streams undulated towards the group. The green light oozed its way around Marguerite and her husband. Suddenly it disappeared and the two fell to the ground unconscious.

"What did you do to them?" Carter cried as he knelt at his grandfather's side. "Grandpa! Wake up!"

Nimue turned to the boy, her eyes like steel knives stabbing into his own. He felt a coldness seep into his chest as the woman continued to stare at him. "What is your power, boy? I know you are afraid."

Carter gulped, then stared back into the woman's eyes, as if he could push her away bodily with his look. "Come, boy. Don't you want to go home to see your mother?" His mother? He recognized the small sphere at Nimue's throat. Had this terrible woman hurt his mother? Was she still alive? His chin trembled as he fought back both tears and anger. "Yes," the honey voice continued. "You are right to be afraid for her. If the spell is not broken soon she will die."

Carter stood. "What spell? What did you do to her?"

Stonehurst, who stood behind and to the left of Nimue, spoke, his eyes burning with his lust for power. "We have the pendant she wore. Lady Nimue put a sleeping spell on her, but at dawn it becomes a spell of death."

"Let her go!" the boy shouted.

Nimue nodded. "I can do that, but only if you and your friends join me. Swear your loyalty to me and your mother will awaken at once." She raised her hand and shaped it as though she would come over and grab his throat. She stood with the Lia Fail before her, the light now pulsing with blood red and black, which swirled around the entire hilltop. Though she did not even approach him, Carter felt a strong, cold grip around his throat. He could not move, nor could he take his eyes off the enchantress as the icy power held him fast.

Merlin took a step forward. "Stop!" he cried.

Nimue laughed. "You come to me with two old weaklings and a couple of children. Do you think you can stop me with such great warriors as those? Truly you have gone mad, old man!" She laughed as Carter's feet left the ground and he rose up into the air. He kicked and struggled against the invisible force. His breath came in short, desperate gasps as he strove to pull in enough air through his constricted windpipe. His hands flailed at whatever grasped his throat, in a vain attempt to free himself.

Merlin turned to face Carter, stretching his hands out towards the powerful stream of energy that threatened to choke the boy. He stood as in a trance, his palms emanating a bright white light that whirled in front of Carter's throat. The boy began to breathe more easily, with less constriction.

"You cannot surpass my power now that I have the sphere, Merlin," Nimue hissed. "You can do no more than help him die a slower death." A cruel smile curled her thin lips as she fixed the boy's eyes with her own. "Unless you decide to become my

125

servant...that is the only way you will find yourself alive in the morning."

Carter closed his eyes to break away from the piercing gaze of the sorceress. His legs hung limp in the air. He focused on breathing, no longer struggling. Calm down, he told himself. With his eyes still closed he put his hands up to feel for the invisible force that held him by the throat. Merlin continued to hold the pressure back so that Carter could breathe.

The woman laughed again. "You will not escape." With her hand still out in front of her holding the boy, Nimue turned her gaze to Penny. The girl tried to close her eyes and turn away. "This is a vision from which you cannot turn away, girl. You can see for yourself what destiny awaits you. You were born for this!"

Penny saw herself at Nimue's side, ordering the deaths of her friends. She clapped her hands over her eyes but the vision trapped her in its horror as she saw ten of the decayed warriors cut down Carter and his grandparents. A scream rang out in the thick air as Penny saw herself take Excalibur and thrust it into the enchanter. The sound ripped out of her throat, "Noooooooo!" She fell to the ground, sobbing. Even with her hands over her eyes, she could only see Merlin's blood running down the sword and spreading in a crimson wave over her clothes.

"That is enough, Nimue." Merlin spoke in firm tones that broke through the girl's vision. Penny gasped and opened her eyes. Carter still hung in the air while Marguerite and Michael lay unmoving where they had fallen. Merlin turned to her. "It's all right, now," he assured her. She nodded, relief flooding her with its welcome balm.

"This..." he began, fixing his gaze on the sorceress, "this is our battle."

Nimue withdrew her hand. Carter fell to the ground in a gasping heap. He put his hands around his neck, which felt bruised from the sorceress's grasp. He could not speak, but only watched helplessly as Merlin took a step toward his old student.

"Let them go. Then you shall have me just where you want me." The enchanter stood before her, his arms out in a gesture of resignation. "Do you so easily forget that I was once your teacher?" he asked softly. "That we shared many happy times together?"

Nimue laughed. "You are quite mistaken in your memories, but I would expect that in such an elderly man. You are not what you used to be, Merlin. Without the power you used to wield, you are no longer a worthy adversary." She gazed with scorn at the old man before her. "I pity you."

"Have you enough of a heart to find pity there, my lady?"

Nimue cocked her head, staring at Merlin for a moment. Her mask softened a little. "Perhaps not, old man. I did not have enough heart to do more than pretend to love you so I could learn your magic, and surpass you in power." The mask hardened; her eyes blazed. "And that is what I have done. I have acquired power greater than yours, enchanter. You have nothing left but parlor tricks, while I..." She looked around the field at the soldiers she had raised then turned back to Merlin, "I have the power to give life...and take it away again."

The woman touched the Lia Fail then gestured to the first rank of the undead warriors. Suddenly the entire rank fell to the ground and sank into the earth. Carter blinked and shook his head. It was not an illusion. The warriors had disappeared. He stood, mostly recovered from Nimue's spell, and watched the drama unfold before him.

"Life?" Merlin asked, a hint of pity in his own voice. "You could not give them life to begin with. Your army is dead. These decaying bodies will return to dust again. They will return to the mass grave in which you found them."

Nimue touched the Lia Fail again. "Watch and see what I do with them, and your pathetic companions. Watching will be all you will be able to do, enchanter, helpless and hopeless, trapped in your own impotence." She raised her hand, fingers extended toward him. "I chose this tree for you, old man," she said sweetly, gesturing with her head to the ancient tree whose branches spread out above them.

Merlin glanced at the trunk of the old yew. Turning his gaze back to the sorceress, he simply shrugged. "It's as good as any place for a retirement, of sorts."

Penny and Carter exchanged a meaningful glance. They each took a step toward their friend. Without even looking at them, Merlin put up a hand to stop them. "No, stay back," he ordered gently. "Let these children go, Nimue. I will not fight you."

The woman laughed, a wild laugh of exultation. "You shall watch them turn against you, from your new prison!" She moved her fingers and a ghastly black-red light streamed lazily from them toward the magician. Merlin's expression did not change. He stood calmly watching the light undulate in his direction. A wisp of black swept in front of the light. Suddenly, Mortimer stood in front of Merlin, shielding the enchanter from the sickly light that crept closer and closer. He turned and threw his pendant around Merlin's neck.

"Uncle Mort!" Carter cried, not knowing if the man had come to help Merlin or Nimue. Mortimer glanced at the boy then stepped into the now swirling dark light. He stood in the light as it engulfed him completely. He gave a battle cry and disappeared.

Nimue stared, open-mouthed in amazement. Her face took on a demonic fury as she reached out to touch the Lia Fail again.

CHAPTER SEVENTEEN
The Stone of Power

The stone rose from its resting place and moved away from the sorceress. "The stone! Who wields this power?" she cried out in a horrifying shriek. She followed the stone, which now began to give off a pure blue-green light. She reached out, intent only on touching it and taking it back.

The stone came to rest in Carter's outstretched hands. He held it at chest level and stared into its sea-green depths. He did not look up as Nimue approached. As she stood before him she grew taller and larger until she towered several feet over the boy. He glanced up at her for a moment, unmoved.

"This stone is mine, boy! Give it to me or you and your friends shall suffer for it!" She reached with huge arms to clutch greedily for the sphere. Her hands moved through it as if she were a ghost. Try as she might, she could not take it from the boy. "Give it to me!" she screamed.

The boy gazed into the sphere as the light within mixed with pure white light and swirled out from the center. He felt removed from everything except the light before him. Carter didn't even raise his voice when he spoke to Nimue. "Back off!" Suddenly, the swirling light shot out of the sphere like a bolt of lightning, crashing into the sorceress and sending her flying back across the top of the hill. She landed at the feet of Stonehurst, whose face had turned the color of old school paste. He clutched his hands together over and over again as he stared at the woman he had served for so many years.

"My lady, get up. Get it back! He's just a boy."

Nimue lay on the ground, stunned from the blow. She shook her huge head and sat up. Glaring at Carter she screamed at him. "How dare you do harm to me. I am Queen! I have the power to kill all of you with the merest touch of my hand!" She rose to her feet, towering even higher over everyone on the hill.

Merlin stood at Carter's side, with Penny at the boy's right. Carter glanced from the huge figure to each of his friends, and then to the sphere. Golden strands of light now wove their way into the swirls of white and a soft blue-green. The colors reminded him of the waters around Bermuda. He had gone there a couple of years ago to visit his mother's sister and her family. Again his thoughts went to his mother, who still slept under Nimue's spell.

"She will be fine," Merlin reassured him. Carter nodded. He turned his gaze on the sorceress. She had raised her huge arms and now gestured to the leading rank of warriors. Their feet fell in dead thuds as they marched up the hill toward them.

"Now what?" Penny asked.

"That is up to Carter now." Merlin put a confident hand on the boy's shoulder.

Carter stood straight and tall, still holding the sphere, as the soldiers advanced toward him. "Okay, now what do I do?" he murmured.

Merlin smiled. "Whatever you want to do, young enchanter."

The boy turned to the old man in surprise. "What I want to do?" Merlin nodded and turned him by the shoulders so he faced the enemy. Carter took a deep breath and took a step forward.

The group of warriors came to a halt just a few feet away from the boy. He could smell the putrid decay of their bodies. The leader raised a huge sword to strike the boy down. Carter saw maggots fall out of the arm that held the sword. He suddenly felt frightened again. How could he stop these horrifying creatures from killing him and his friends?

The light in the sphere grew brighter, swirling with gold and white light. Carter stared into the ball, remembering how its light had struck Nimue back from him, even in her gigantic form. He looked again at the warrior before him. The sword began its downward swing, as if in slow motion. "Stop!" Carter cried. The warrior froze. A maggot hung in the air, in the middle of its fall from the soldier's arm.

What did he want to do with them? They had to be returned to their resting place, but how? Nimue approached, her hand out toward the decayed man. A reddish-brown light shot from her fingers and oozed into the warrior's chest. "Kill him now!" she ordered.

The maggot fell to the ground as the sword swung back up into the air above Carter's head. The boy stood firmly rooted to the spot. He focused on the sphere and imagined the soldier turning to dust and disappearing into the ground. A blast of white light shot from the ball and into the man's chest. "No!" Nimue cried. With both of her huge hands she sent another stream of ugly color into the warrior.

Carter concentrated more intently on the sphere. The light whirled out of it and completely enveloped the soldier before him. The dead man's eyes lit up with the light. It poured out of his hands, head, and feet. A face, rugged and battle-worn, appeared in the place of the decayed, partly skeletal face of the grotesque warrior. It turned and glared at Nimue. Fear splashed across her features before they fell back into a livid mask. She poured more of the sickly dark light into the man, but his form took on a brightness that made her squint and turn her face to the side.

The brilliant face turned to Carter. A deep but gentle voice rolled from the bright soldier. "Let us go now, young master. Let us go back to our rest."

Carter nodded. "If I can set you free from this spell, I will."

Nimue screamed again. "No! That is not in your power! You are a child holding a tool you cannot possibly understand or control." She took a step towards him.

Carter's heart fluttered in his chest. He took a deep breath and let it out slowly to calm himself. He returned to his relaxed, trancelike state. As he looked over at the sorceress he could see the fear in her eyes despite her best efforts to hide it. Turning his gaze on the warrior before him, he spoke in firm tones. "Return, then. Return to your rest."

"Thank you." The soldier inclined his head in respect toward the boy. He straightened and turned back to his men. "Let us go now. We have been granted leave to return." In unison the men turned around and marched down the hill. As each man stepped

131

onto the level ground at the bottom of the hill, they sank into the earth until all had disappeared.

"So you could get rid of a few of them," Nimue began. "I still rule the rest." The sorceress pointed at Excalibur. The sword leapt into her hand. It looked like no more than a small dagger in proportion to the gigantic woman. She moved her huge form to the edge of the hilltop. Raising the sword in her right hand over the mass of decaying men before her, she spoke. "I am still your Queen."

Blood red light began to glow from the sword. It spilled over the entire hilltop, yet could not extinguish the light from the great sphere. "Come up here and kill this boy!" Nimue commanded in a wrathful voice.

Silence answered her words. The soldiers stood in place, not even shuffling their feet. "Hear me!" the sorceress cried, a hint of panic edging into her voice. "Come kill these people! They are your enemies!"

Still the men stood in silence, unmovable. Excalibur now gave off an oily, brownish-red light. It ran from the tip of the sword down to its hilt and dripped onto the ground at Nimue's feet. A sudden flash of red-orange light shone from the center of the blade. Now the sword looked like it was nothing more than molten steel. Nimue shrieked in pain and dropped it on the ground. The steel writhed in the grass, melting into a twisted mass of metal. Excalibur was no more. Merlin sighed and lowered his hand.

Carter carried the brilliant sphere to the edge of the hill. As the light poured out upon the soldiers, Nimue screamed in fury, but dared not move closer to the boy. He raised the sphere and called out to the ranks of decaying men. "Warriors. The battle is over."

Each man watched the boy, as though listening very carefully. Their faces began to glow and Carter saw the men as they were on the day they had all died. He remembered the words of their leader. "I grant you leave to return to your rest!" The entire field lit up, not only with white light, but also with radiant colors of the rainbow. The soldiers became transparent as the living people on the hill watched in wonder.

Nimue stepped back from the sight, shielding her eyes with her hands. She cried out to any that would listen, but the sounds bounced back to her as if they had hit a wall.

Michael awoke and stood up to see the beautiful light. He glanced toward his wife, who had also awakened from the power of the spell. He walked to her and helped her to her feet. Together they moved to Merlin's side to watch the warriors sink into the ground as the pure light swirled in dazzling patterns around the field before them. Penny smiled up at the Griffins then turned her head to continue watching the spectacle.

The light began to fade quickly where the soldiers had once stood. Finally it disappeared and left the field in darkness. The hilltop remained bright, however, still illuminated by the large sphere. Carter lowered the Lia Fail to chest level again. He turned to Merlin. His face glowed with an otherworldly light. He grinned when he saw his grandparents. Their eyes shone with love and pride in their grandson's gifts. The boy moved toward the group, relieved that the whole frightening nightmare had ended at last. He shifted the ball to one arm while he hugged his grandparents, and then Penny. Carter turned to Merlin, who stopped him with a sharp look.

The enchanter turned his eyes to Nimue. Carter followed his gaze. Nimue! How could he have forgotten that she could still pose a danger to them? The sorceress glared at him, growing even taller than she had before. "So, you think it's all over and you can go home after your little adventure." The woman's face twisted into a cruel smile. "Think again, boy."

The sphere felt heavy in his hands. Carter wondered why he hadn't noticed the weight before then. The light dwindled to a small sparkle in the middle of the ball, casting the hill into semi-darkness. The group could still see by the light of the waxing moon and the stars that shone clearly in the silken night sky.

Penny ran a calculating gaze over the sorceress. She noticed that she could see the stars through Nimue's body. Merlin glanced down at the girl. They exchanged a meaningful look.

Carter felt fear begin to grasp at him again. His heart beat hard and fast now. He looked from the monstrous form of Nimue to the heavy sphere in his hands. Now the light had gone out completely. As Nimue took a step toward him he turned to Merlin, pushing the ball into the enchanter's hands.

"Take it, please!" he whispered. "It will be safer with you." Merlin nodded, taking the lightless sphere and putting it into his robes where it seemed to disappear.

Nimue stopped her advance and cried, "What have you done with it, Merlin?" Her voice softened. "Think of the power we could share." The old man gazed steadily at her. "Yes, you and I could share its power. We could be together as we once were. We could rule as one, you and I." As the woman stooped and reached out to him she began to shrink in size until she returned to her normal height. "You and me—just the two of us together, in love and...power." The honeyed tones seemed to hold the enchanter in their spell. He did not take his eyes off Nimue. "Come, my love. Take out the sphere and give it to me."

Merlin's hand edged toward his robe. His friends watched in stunned silence. Suddenly Penny grabbed his arm and shouted, "No! Don't do it!"

He turned a smile on the girl as he gently took her hand from his arm, reached into his robe and brought out the Lia Fail. A tiny swirl of light moved slowly within its depths. He held it out to Nimue. "Take it, then, my love."

The woman's features took on a soft, feminine look. "I promise we will be together forever." Watching the old enchanter's face, she reached out to touch the sphere. Her hands stopped in mid-air. She tried to grasp at the ball, but her hands met an invisible barrier. She flailed at the sphere, her hands bouncing off a couple of inches away from it.

"It would seem that you cannot take the stone," Merlin commented with a wry smile. "Not even from an old man who has nothing left but...what did you say? Ah, yes, nothing left but parlor tricks."

Nimue faced him, struggling to maintain her composure. "I spoke wrongly of you. I know you are still a powerful mage." Her eyes took on a crafty glint. "Why else would I invite you to share power with me? We can rule the world together. We can—"

"No," the enchanter interrupted.

Penny's face seemed about to explode unless she could speak her mind. "Of course he's not going to rule with you! He's not like you at all. He's not obsessed with ruling the world like you are, and he's sure not stupid enough to think you'd actually let him!" She gestured toward the yew trunk. "You put him in a tree once before, and you just told him a few minutes ago that you'd put him in that one! Are you brain-dead?" She took another breath to continue.

Merlin raised a hand to stop the girl's tirade. A smile twinkled in his clear blue eyes. "It is a nicer tree, …but I have other plans." The sorceress backed away from Merlin. Drawing herself to her full height, she thrust out her right hand at him while with her left she touched the small sphere at her throat. "I hold her life here. Look!" She grasped the pendant and pulled hard. The silver chain broke. The woman dangled the tiny globe in front of them. She turned her gaze on Carter, a wild half-smile playing over her features.

The small, clear globe transfixed the boy's gaze. As he watched, his heart seemed to twist itself into knots. The sphere grew cloudy with white mist that darkened into gray. "What are you doing?" Carter whispered.

"Now you show respect, boy. Maybe it is too late for that now. Maybe…" Nimue glared at him. The smile had turned cruel again. "Maybe I will kill her now…before the sun rises, before you have a chance to rescue her…"

The boy's lips trembled as he tried to speak. "W—why…would you do that?" Penny put an arm around his shoulders. This time she held her tongue.

"Why should I not?" the sorceress returned sweetly. "You have taken my victory away from me. There are consequences. There are always consequences."

Merlin turned his gaze from Nimue to the boy beside him. "Carter," he said softly. The boy looked up into the enchanter's kind face. He stood silently, waiting for the wise old man to continue his thought. But Merlin said nothing more as he held the great sphere out for Carter to take.

"What is this for? Don't give this to me." Carter covered his eyes with his hands for a moment. When he took them away from his face he saw that the enchanter still held the sphere out for him.

"Yes," Nimue hissed. "I might trade your mother's life for that."

Carter turned his eyes to the small sphere in Nimue's hand. The gray clouds took on a darker, more foreboding shade. Nimue nodded. "You don't have much time. When the sphere turns black your mother dies."

The Lia Fail began to glow next to the boy. He glanced from its pure, golden light to the sorceress. His mother's sphere had turned a dark brown. He looked into Merlin's compassionate eyes. "Please tell me what to do," he whispered urgently.

"This is something I cannot decide for you. Your course of action could very well change the world. Or maybe there are more choices than you think." The enchanter winked at him.

Carter stopped shaking. Had he actually seen Merlin wink at him? Why would he do that when so much was at stake? He nodded slowly at the old man then turned to face the sorceress. The small globe was almost black. He held out his hand, speaking in firm tones. "That belongs to my mother. Give it to me."

Nimue took a step toward him. "Take it," she dared.

The boy's other hand reached out to touch the Lia Fail as its light grew brighter. He would blast the sorceress back as he had done before.

"No, don't," Penny whispered urgently beside him. With a cry she sprang at the woman, knocking her to the ground. The sphere flew out of Nimue's hand and high into the air.

Carter didn't take his eyes off the sphere as he moved into position and held up his hand to catch it. Like a pop fly ball back home the pendant dropped right into his hand. He clutched it to his chest for a moment, relief rushing through him like a great stream flooding a dry plain.

Penny had knocked the wind out of the sorceress, who lay on the dark grass gasping for breath. The girl stood up and brushed some dirt off her jeans. She hurried to Carter's side as he opened his hand to look at the small globe. The dark brown had already changed back to gray, but the sphere did not lighten any more than that.

Carter caught Merlin's gaze as he, too, studied the ball. "What does it mean?"

"It means..." Nimue rose to her feet, her features set in her cruel mask. "It means that you will be too late to save her." She nodded slowly. "It means your mother will die despite your futile struggle to save her."

136

Carter looked from the sorceress to the sphere in horror. Merlin spoke quickly. "It's not too late. She wants you to despair. Look to the horizon. The sun will rise soon here, but not for five more hours at your aunt's house."

The boy glanced up, hope now shining in his eyes. Merlin put a hand on the back of his neck and gently turned him toward the crest of the hill. "You must go now. She will be difficult to awaken, even now." He gave him a light push.

"Thanks," Carter called over his shoulder as he began to run down the hill to the portal. His grandparents hurried after him. Marguerite snatched her sphere from its silk pouch at her waist and held it up to set the portal in motion. Purple light swirled out of the archway as they each ran into it and disappeared.

Penny, who still stood at the enchanter's side, watched them go. She turned her eyes back to Nimue. The woman's face was contorted with rage, its flesh red with fury, as she glared at Merlin and the girl. For a moment she could not even speak. When she finally found her voice, Merlin had already returned the Lia Fail to his robe. He turned to walk over to the trunk of the ancient yew. He did not pause as the woman sputtered out her wrath.

"You—you will not win this time! I controlled you once before and I will control you again!" She continued to yell at him, but the enchanter paid no heed. Penny followed the old man to stand beside him in front of the tree.

Merlin shook his head. "I'm not sure if he is even in here." He placed his hands on the bark, feeling around for something.

"What are you looking for?" the girl asked.

"Carter's great uncle."

"Uncle Mort? Why are you looking here, in a tree? Besides, didn't he come to help Nimue?"

Merlin smiled down at Penny, her face covered with scratches, mud and blood from their battles. "My dear, brave girl, Mortimer shielded me from her spell. It was meant to entrap me in this tree." He took a hand away from the trunk and held up the pendant Carter's uncle had thrown around his neck just before he stepped into the sickly light of the spell.

"This is the talisman he carried in his antique box that day back at the house." He shook his head. "I did not know he had it. I really had no idea where his loyalties lay—with me or Nimue or if he was in this just for himself. Power tempts even the best of us."

Penny reached out to touch the pendant. She ran her finger along the carved surface, recognizing the notched symbols in the early morning light. "This looks a lot like the Ogham symbols on the door of the Chamber of Art."

"Yes. This has been in the Feltree family since Linus made it, after he rescued me from the forest. In every generation of the Feltree family a new guardian was appointed for me. The talisman was meant to protect the guardian from spells."

"That way no one could get at the door," Penny guessed as she looked up at Merlin. He nodded and turned back to the tree.

Penny glanced over at Nimue. She had ceased screaming at Merlin. Now Stonehurst stood at the woman's side, a comforting arm around her shoulders. Suddenly the sorceress shook off the arm and stalked down the hill toward the portal.

Penny turned to the enchanter and grabbed his sleeve. "Nimue is heading for the sphere over the portal."

Merlin did not stop moving his hands over the bark. "Don't worry," he answered absently. "Carter's grandfather put a shield around it just as they left. She can't get to it now."

Penny watched as Stonehurst followed the sorceress. The two stood before the archway. Nimue must have ordered him to get the sphere because Stonehurst clambered up the side of the portal and reached out for the stone. He pulled his hand away quickly as sparks jumped out of it and burned his fingers. He scurried back down to Nimue, who screamed something at him. He cowered before her, shaking his head and blowing on his injured fingers.

"Ah, I think I have found him." Merlin smiled triumphantly as he settled his hands over a spot on the tree. "Yes, there he is."

Penny cocked her head and gazed at the trunk as the old man began to sweep his hands over the spot. As the enchanter worked the girl saw the wood become clear as though it were a window into the heart of the tree. She took a step closer to see what Merlin had uncovered. Penny gasped. "It's him! It's Uncle Mort!"

Merlin nodded. Mortimer stood inside the tree behind what looked like thick glass. His eyes fluttered open. His features remained calm as Merlin reached into the tree and began to slowly pull him out. Mort tried to take a step and stumbled out of the tree into Merlin's arms. "I seem to not have the use of my legs," the pale man whispered as he clung to Merlin. Though Mortimer tried he could not bear any weight on his legs.

"Don't let that trouble you, Feltree. You will be able to walk in a few moments." Merlin set him gently in the grass. "Rest here for now."

Mortimer tried to rise again, muttering, "The last sphere. We have to get the last sphere or Nimue will—"

"She cannot get it," Merlin interrupted. He pointed down the hill to the two figures standing in the bright purple and white light of the portal. Nimue clambered up the side of the arch and reached for the sphere. Sparks flew out of it at her fingers. Jerking them back, the woman shook the pain from her hand and tried again. This time the globe shocked her so hard she fell from her perch. Nimue got up and shook her fists at the offensive object.

Penny burst out laughing, so loudly that Nimue turned to look at her. Stamping her feet, she shook a fist at the three on the hilltop.

Penny grinned. "You know, from here she looks a lot like an angry cockroach."

"Yes," the enchanter nodded, his eyes twinkling with mirth, "very much like that particular household pest."

A thin smile brightened Mortimer's pallid features. Merlin looked down at him and held out his hand. "Let's see how those legs work now, my dear Feltree." Mortimer took the old man's hand. The enchanter pulled him to his feet. He swayed slightly as he took his first few steps. The enchanter held his arm and gently walked him several paces. Soon Mortimer's gait returned to its normal, casual grace. The three walked over to where Excalibur lay in a tangled mass of fused metal. Only the beautiful, gem-studded hilt remained unscathed. Merlin stooped to pick it up. He straightened, turning the ruined sword over in his hands.

"Why did you have to destroy Excalibur?" Penny asked.

"The sword had already been corrupted when Nimue used it to raise the dead warriors from their grave. It was a sword of light, a sword of knowledge." Merlin shook his head. "To be turned to such evil destroyed its original purpose, and hence the sword itself."

Mortimer reached out and rubbed his finger over part of the twisted blade, revealing the shining metal beneath the darkened surface. He glanced at Merlin. The enchanter smiled. "Perhaps it is not lost to us forever." He put it away in his robe and turned to stride down the hill.

Penny looked at Mortimer. "What did he mean by that?" she asked.

Carter's uncle put a thin hand on her shoulder. "I don't really know, but with Merlin...well, nothing should surprise us." They followed the enchanter to the portal.

"You," Nimue spat as she pointed at Merlin. "You will taste my revenge, yet, old man."

As Merlin put up a hand to quiet her, a look of fear crept over the woman's face. She glanced back and forth from his face to his hand, as if she expected him to do her harm. "Come with us back to Avalon." Merlin turned his gaze to the shaking Stonehurst. "And you, too, Henry."

The fearful man glanced from Merlin to Nimue. Her dark eyes threatened punishment, "You cannot leave me now, Henry. You know what will happen if you even try. Besides, I am not finished yet."

"N—n—no, of course not," but Stonehurst looked doubtful.

The light in the portal grew brighter. Merlin and his companions turned toward it. The enchanter looked back at Nimue and her servant once more. "The guardians can help you both find a better way to live."

"You know nothing of how I want to live. You were always an old fool," Nimue cried over the whirring sounds of the pulsating light.

Merlin put his hands on his friends' shoulders. "Then we must take our leave of you both." He gave his friends a gentle push. "After you, my dears." The two stepped into the light and disappeared.

Suddenly Nimue scrambled up the side of the arch and scrabbled desperately for the sphere, which shocked her several times before it finally came loose and dropped straight into Merlin's hand. He held it up as the sorceress cursed at him. "Why, thank you," he answered, ignoring the stream of foul language. A mischievous look crossed his face. "Yes, this is the greatest service you have done for me today." With that Merlin stepped into the light and disappeared.

Perched on the top of the arch, Nimue shrieked in unbearable anger and frustration. Her screams echoed around the field. Then, their tones changed and became the cries of a large raven that flapped its dark wings and flew away. Henry Stonehurst watched her go then raised his arms. From the spot where he had stood a second raven took off and followed the other into the distant trees.

CHAPTER EIGHTEEN
Return Home

The portal took Carter and his grandparents back to the Chamber of Art. The three of them ran all the way down the long corridors to the parlor of the old mansion. The boy's mother lay on the floor in front of the divan. He hurried to kneel beside her. She was still breathing, but her breaths were slow and shallow. Her face was pale.

"Mom!" Carter cried as he shook her shoulders with urgency. "Mom! Wake up!" She continued to lie still, but now she breathed more deeply.

"Clarice!" Marguerite knelt down and began massaging her daughter's head, neck and shoulders. "Wake up, sweetheart. You have to get up now!"

Slowly the younger woman stirred. Her eyes fluttered open. "Wh—what's going on? Mom! Dad! We thought you were dead!"

Michael moved to his daughter's side, a look of relief flooding his rugged features. "No, Clarice, we are very much alive." Kneeling on the floor he helped his daughter sit up. A tear rolled down his cheek as he held her in his arms.

"I've missed you and Mom so much!" Clarice wept freely as she turned to embrace her mother.

Marguerite held her tightly. "We missed you and the family more than I can say."

The Griffins helped their daughter up onto the divan. Clarice sat up, wiping her tear stained face on her sleeve.

She smiled at her parents and at her son, who seemed to have grown slightly taller than the last time she had seen him. Mrs. Blume noticed a new confidence in his look. Usually he only took on that look during baseball games. "Carter." She held out her arms. Carter bent down and hugged his mom tightly. She kissed him on the cheek before letting him straighten up again.

"We just got back from England," Carter began excitedly. "We were in Avalon and saw King Arthur, but he was still sleeping and there were these horrible dead guys that we had to fight and—"

Clarice held up a hand and shook her head as if to clear it. "One thing at a time. All I remember was that rude old woman with her servant." She closed her eyes, trying to remember. "Miss Nimway...and...Stonehurst... They barged in the door like they owned the place. She stared at me... I felt very strange. I'm not sure how I got in here, and..." She reached up to her throat. "My pendant—she must have taken it." She tried to get up but her father gently pushed her back down to her seat.

"You need not worry." Michael gently took her face in his hands for a moment. "It's over now." Clarice nodded and relaxed a little.

Carter sat down on the edge of the divan next to his mother. He held out his hand. "Here it is, Mom."

Clarice gazed from her son's face to the sphere he held in his hand. A twinkle of light shone from its center. She reached for it and held it up for a moment. Looking into her son's eyes she nodded slowly in understanding. "Thank you," she told Carter in little more than a whisper.

"No problem." Carter's voice caught in his throat.

Marguerite turned to her grandson. "How did you know how to bring the Lia Fail to you? Such telekinetic power does not usually develop in one so young."

The boy grinned sheepishly. "I don't really know what happened. One minute I was standing next to Penny, and the next I found myself in front of the stone. Once I picked it up I was back where I'd started, with the sphere in my hands."

Suddenly, Carter heard the sound of quick steps down the long hall to the right of the staircase. "Someone's coming." The boy looked to his grandparents. Michael had already moved to where the room opened on the hallway to peer around the corner. Marguerite stood beside him, ready with her sphere glowing in her hand. The steps came closer and a familiar voice rolled down the hall. "It's all right. We are not here to do battle." With that, Merlin strode into the parlor, followed by Penny and Mortimer.

Michael reached out and clasped the enchanter's hand. "So, all must be well in Avalon."

"The Lia Fail has been returned and the city is now quite safe," Merlin said with a satisfied smile. Marguerite moved to Mortimer's side and hugged her brother close. "I thought we might have lost you."

"Only for a little while," he answered, his eyes warm with affection.

Clarice stared at the old man in his flowing purple and white robes. "Are you...I thought you were some old hippie when I saw you first."

Merlin grinned. " Good. I was rather pleased with that look myself." He winked at her. "I should like to try it again, sometime. It's an expressive style."

"So," Clarice began, "You aren't a leftover from the sixties..."

The enchanter laughed kindly at her look of confusion. "No, more like a leftover from the five hundreds."

"I had heard of you before, from my mother." She stood and held out her hand to the magician.

He took it gently in his own, saying, "Yes, your mother told me that you had chosen not to receive the complete training. You wished to marry and raise children 'in a normal world.' I believe those were your exact words." Clarice blushed and opened her mouth to speak. Merlin raised his hand to stop her. "That is a wonderful way to live, my dear. But you should know that training is available to you at any time you might wish it; such is your inheritance."

She nodded. "Thank you, Merlin."

"I have some questions for all of you." Marguerite stood straight with her hands on her hips. Everyone turned to face her. "I understand that my sister, Belinda, kept us in Avalon with a spell, but...where were you, Mortimer, when we came to see you? And why did you pass the guardianship over to her?"

Carter's uncle looked down to study the floor, an embarrassed expression on his usually pale face. "The fact is...I didn't. Early one morning I heard her in the basement. Suspecting that thoughts of power may have affected her judgment, I hurried down to the door and caught her performing a spell to release Lord Merlin from the door. Before I could even say a word, she trapped me in one of those garden gargoyles. It was only from her magical diary that I learned my suspicions were correct." He looked up at the enchanter. "I'm sorry for failing you. I should have been able to stop her."

The old man gazed fondly at Mortimer. "You never failed me." Mort nodded uncertainly.

Penny cocked her head, "Now I understand why you came to the Chamber of Art for the book. But we heard you in there again. Merlin said you were scrying."

"Yes," Mortimer began with a twinkle in his eye. "I thought there were some uninvited visitors to the chamber...on both occasions." He continued, his voice serious again. "I had read about the spell cast on my sister and her husband." He gestured to Carter's grandparents, who both looked quite surprised at what Belinda had done.

"I thought they would still be in Avalon. The scrying mirror confirmed that, but also showed me that the city was in imminent danger. I knew I had to find a way there. When I found the door and could not feel the enchanter's presence, I realized that these gifted children had somehow released him."

Penny blushed. "We thought you wanted to catch Merlin and put him back in the door."

"I did not take you into my confidence as, perhaps, I should have done. Instead, I followed you to make sure Merlin had, indeed, found his freedom, and also so I could go back through the portal when the enchanter returned to Avalon, as I knew he would."

"How did you know that?" Carter asked.

The pale man tapped his head. "If I could see the danger, then I was sure that Merlin would see it, too. He would use his sphere to activate the portal and I could go with you, possibly undetected in its powerful energies."

"And you almost were," the enchanter began. "I must admit I was...uncertain of your loyalties until I saw you enter the portal with us to follow Nimue's warriors."

"That's what the black smoke was about," Carter exclaimed.

Uncle Mort turned in surprise. "Then you saw it, too?"

"Well, yeah."

"So did I," Penny added.

Merlin chuckled. "It seems, my dear fellow, that you need to review your invisibility lessons."

Clarice glanced around at the group. "I'm afraid you're going to have to start from the beginning with me. Apparently, I have missed everything."

Marguerite took her daughter's hand and started toward the kitchen. "I don't know about all of you but I'm starving. Let's get something to eat—pizza's on me!"

"Sounds great, Mrs. Griffin. Do you use magic for that?" Penny asked.

Marguerite reached into her back pocket, pulled out a slim wallet and held it up. "I think this little object should work that magic."

The girl laughed. "Then we really are back home."

* * * * *

Pizza had never tasted so good to Carter. Maybe there was magic in it or maybe the stories and the closeness of his family and friends made it special. At any rate, they all sat or stood around the kitchen until well past dawn, telling Mrs. Blume about their adventures. When the last tale had been told Merlin spoke. "Yes, our two youngsters proved themselves more than worthy of their heritage."

The boy's features took on a downcast look. "I wasn't very brave at the end. It was just that...that I suddenly got scared."

"When we are fearless we have no need of courage. But when we are afraid...that is when we need courage the most." Merlin looked deeply into Carter's eyes. "I knew you were about to strike Nimue with the light again." The enchanter patted him on the back. "Your fiery-tempered friend intervened because she saw something that you, and I, did not."

Penny blushed. "I saw your mom killed by a flash of light from the sphere. I had to stop you and Nimue. Besides," she added with a sly smile, "I knew I could take her."

146

Merlin gazed at Carter and Penny in turn, admiration in his eyes. "The two of you have also proven that you are ready to receive training in the ancient arts, if you so desire."

"That would be so cool!" The boy could hardly stand still at this exciting news.

"You mean I can learn how to do magic?" Penny asked, not daring to believe Merlin's words.

"Absolutely," the enchanter replied. "However, at this age there is one more requirement." The two friends held their breath, waiting for Merlin's next words. "You must have your parents' permission."

Carter looked over at his mother, who smiled and nodded. "Your father will not be surprised. We both know of your telekinetic gift. After all, baseballs don't usually change directions so they can fall into the outfielder's hand."

The boy's face glowed with happiness. He breathed in the scents of pizza, root beer, and the usual smell of the mansion, which no longer reminded him of his great aunt. Instead, the old house had become a place of daring adventure and exciting revelations.

Penny interrupted his thoughts. "Race you to my house!"

"But it's so early," he answered, almost hearing his aunt's voice in his tone.

"My parents are usually up by now. I've got to ask them about learning magic." Penny laughed and pulled the kitchen door open. "You coming?"

Carter glanced at his mom. She nodded. "You bet I am," he cried, and followed her out of the door into a new day.

Printed in the United States
22413LVS00001B/280-294

9 780974 408439